DOCTOR PROCTOR'S
FART
POWDER

THE GREAT GOLD
ROBBERY

Also by Jo Nesbø

Doctor Proctor's Fart Powder

Doctor Proctor's Fart Powder:
Time-Travel Bath Bomb

Doctor Proctor's Fart Powder:
The End of the World. Maybe

Doctor Proctor's Fart Powder:
Can Doctor Proctor Save Christmas?

DOCTOR PROCTOR'S FART POWDER

THE GREAT GOLD ROBBERY

JO NESBØ

SIMON & SCHUSTER

First published in Great Britain in 2013 by Simon and Schuster UK Ltd
A CBS COMPANY

First published in the USA in 2013 by Aladdin,
an imprint of Simon & Schuster Children's Publishing Division
as *Doctor Proctor's Fart Powder: The Magical Fruit*

This edition published in Great Britain in 2018 by Simon & Schuster UK Ltd

Originally published in Norway in 2012 as
Doktor Proktor og det store gullrøveriet by H. Aschehoug & Co.

Text copyright © H. Aschehoug & Co. 2012. Published by arrangement
with the Salomonsson Agency
English translation copyright © 2013 Tara Chace
Interior illustrations copyright © 2013 Mike Lowery

3 5 7 9 10 8 6 4 2

Simon & Schuster UK Ltd
1st Floor, 222 Gray's Inn Road
London WC1X 8HB

Simon & Schuster Australia, Sydney
Simon & Schuster India, New Delhi

A CIP catalogue record for this book is available from the British Library.

PB ISBN: 978-1-4711-7983-9
eBook ISBN: 978-1-4711-1739-8

Printed and bound by CPI Group (UK) Ltd, Croydon, CR0 4YY

www.simonandschuster.co.uk
www.simonandschuster.com.au

DOCTOR PROCTOR'S FART POWDER

THE GREAT GOLD ROBBERY

The Not-Quite-So-Great Gold Robbery

IT IS NIGHTTIME in Oslo, and it's raining on the quiet, sleeping city. Or *is* it sleeping? One of the raindrops hits the enormous clock on the side of the Oslo City Hall tower and clings to the tip of the minute hand before letting go and falling twenty stories, striking the asphalt with a soft splat, and starting to join the other raindrops running down the streetcar tracks. Now, if we were to follow this raindrop as it made its way to a manhole cover during this Oslo night, we would hear a faint sound through the silence. The faint sound would get a little louder when the drop of water fell through the hole in the manhole cover, plunging down into the Oslo sewer system, where the darkness is even thicker. And along with the raindrop we would start sailing in the filthy, reeking sewage water, through the pipes— some small and narrow, some so big you can stand up—that run this way and that, way below ground level in this rather insignificant, big, little city, which is the capital of Norway. And as this intestinal system of pipes carries us deeper into Oslo's innards, the sound gets louder.

It is not a pleasant sound. Actually, it sounds like a dentist's office.

Like the sound of a drill crushing its way through

tooth enamel, gums, and sensitive nerve endings. Sometimes the rumbling is low and sometimes screeching high, depending on what the drill's diamond-hard, whirling bit is digging into.

But, whatever! At least it's not the sound of an anaconda's hissing, yard-long tongue, the creaking of half a ton of constrictor muscles tightening, or the deafening bang of jaws—the size of an inflatable swimming ring—slamming shut on their victim. I only mention that because of the rumor that a snake like that lives down here. And because a pair of yellow, glowing reptilian eyes are just visible in the sewer there in the darkness to the left. So if you are regretting having come already, now's your chance to vamoose. Just quietly close the book and tiptoe out of the room or crawl under the covers. Forget that you ever heard of the Oslo sewer system, that dentist's drill sound, or snakes that eat enormous water voles, average-sized kids, and occasionally small adult humans—if they're not too hairy and don't have beards.

SO, GOOD-BYE AND have a good life. And close the door behind you.

THERE. NOW IT'S just us.

WE WILL CONTINUE down this filthy river toward the dark heart of the city. By now the noise has grown to a roar and we see a light, but we realize that this is neither paradise nor the dentist from hell, but something totally different.

There is a loud machine in front of us with a wheel on it. A steel arm juts up from the machine and disappears into a large hole that has been drilled in the top of the sewer pipe.

"We're almost there, boys!" says the biggest of the three men standing around the machine, shining flashlights up into the hole. They're all dressed the same in black leather boots, rolled-up jeans with suspenders, and white T-shirts. The biggest one also had a bowler hat on his head. But he's taken it off right now to wipe the sweat away, allowing us to see that all three of their heads are shaved, and each one has a letter tattooed on his forehead, above his thick unibrow.

A small cracking sound is heard, and suddenly the drill starts squealing like a spoiled brat.

"We're in," the man with a *B* tattooed on his forehead snarls, flipping a switch. The drilling noise slowly fades away. The drill bit comes into view, and it's quite a sight: It glitters in the light from the flashlights like the biggest diamond in the world. And, well, that's probably because it *is* the biggest diamond in the world, newly stolen from a diamond mine in South Africa.

The guy with a *C* tattooed on his forehead angles a ladder up into the hole above them and scampers up its rungs.

The other two guys watch him anxiously.

For five seconds absolutely nothing happens.

"Charlie?" the guy with the bowler hat calls.

Nothing happens for three more seconds.

Then Charlie comes back into view. He is struggling to carry something that looks like a brick, except that it's golden and obviously much heavier. The side is engraved with some words: BANK OF NORWAY.

And below that, in slightly smaller letters: GOLD BAR NUMBER 101.

"Help me, Betty," Charlie says, and the man with the *B* tattoo hurries over and takes the gold bar.

"What about the rest of them?" the guy with the bowler hat asks, blowing dust off it. He has an *A* tattooed on his forehead, but it's a little hard to read right now since a massive wrinkle is curling the whole letter.

"This is all there is, Alfie."

"What?"

Now, I'm sure at this point the most geographically

astute of you are wondering why these three are speaking English. After all, we are in the sewers beneath Oslo, which is the capital of Norway, and don't people speak Norwegian there? Sadly for those of us who don't understand Norwegian, most of the characters in this book will actually be speaking Norwegian. Happily, we will simply pretend we took one of Doctor Proctor's multilingual pills. But in this specific case that wasn't even necessary. For some reason these three are already speaking English.

"This was the only bar in there, Alfie. The rest of the bank vault is completely empty," Charlie says.

"You mean this is it? The entire gold reserve of the whole darned central bank of Norway?" sputters Betty, the medium-sized one, and then drops the gold

 bar with a thump into the machine's baggage compartment.

"Calm down, Betty," Alfie says. "It looks good, this one. Pure, solid gold all the way through. We'd better be getting home, boys."

"Shh!" Charlie exclaims. "Did you guys hear that sound?"

"What sound?"

"That hissing sound," Charlie says.

"There's no hissing in the sewers, Charlie," Alfie groans. "Rats squeaking and frogs croaking, maybe, but you've got to head farther into the jungle to hear hissing."

"Look!" Charlie says urgently.

"Look at what?" Alfie says.

"Didn't you guys see that? Yellow eyes! They blinked and disappeared," Charlie says.

"Red rat tails and green frog thighs, maybe," says Alfie. "But yellow eyes, you've got to head farther into the jung—"

He is interrupted by a deafening bang.

"Hmm," says Alfie, rubbing his chin. "Maybe we are in the jungle, boys, because that sounded undeniably like snake jaws slamming shut, if you ask me. And I think you'd better ask me. Now!"

"All right, Alfie," Charlie says with a sigh. "Were those snake jaws?"

"Yup. And Mom said she wanted us to bring her something nice from Oslo. How about a boa constrictor?"

"Yippee!" squeals Betty, pulling a heavy, metal F16 out of the baggage compartment. All right, fine. It turns out it isn't an F16 at all. It's an M16. He loads it and starts firing away. The muzzle flash from the machine gun lights up the sewer as the bullets whistle and pop in the sewer pipe.

The other two point their flashlights toward where Charlie saw the yellow eyes. But there's nothing to see, just a trembling rat standing on its hind legs, pressing its back against the wall.

"Rats!" whispers Betty.

"We got what we came for," says Alfie, putting on his bowler hat. "Pack it in. Let's go."

And as we follow the drop of water farther down the sewer pipe toward the treatment plant and the Oslo Fjord, we hear Alfie, Betty, and Charlie packing their equipment back into the machine and starting it up.

But the last thing we hear is . . . ?

You guessed it.

Sssnake hisssssing.

The Secret Guard
Takes the Case

AT PRECISELY EIGHT o'clock in the morning, the governor of Norway's central bank, the Bank of Norway, did what he usually did every morning when he got to work. He walked downstairs to the deepest basement in Norway. He walked past the royal mint where they stamp pictures of the king onto the coins, on down past the presses where they print pictures of famous dead Norwegians—mostly with mustaches—onto the bills, and all the way on down to where people keep their safety-deposit boxes. From there, the bank governor and the deputy governor unlocked and entered all three of the steel doors until they were finally standing in front of the vault containing the entire gold reserves of the nation of Norway.

The bank governor issued his usual command: "Unlock it!"

"Uh, you've got the key, Tor," the deputy governor responded as usual, and then yawned.

"Oh yeah, that's right," the bank governor said as usual, and unlocked the door.

Then they entered the vault.

At exactly four minutes and thirteen seconds after eight, a heartbroken wail was heard from the deepest basement in Norway. And it was exactly four minutes and fifteen seconds after eight when the bank governor whispered to the deputy governor, "Not a word of this to anyone, understand? We mustn't panic now."

"But—but the gold reserve is scheduled to be inspected next Monday!" came the deputy governor's despairing response. "What's going to happen to us? What's going to happen to Norway?"

"Just leave it to me," Bank Governor Tor said.

"What are you going to do?"

Bank Governor Tor thought for a bit and replied, "Panic."

Then they both screamed.

IT WAS NINE o'clock in the morning, and the king was lying in bed as usual, watching the sports news on TV. On the screen the reporter pushed his glasses into place and reported there were rumors that the fabulously wealthy Maximus Rublov, owner of England's Chelchester City soccer team, was going to try to buy Ibranaldovez, the world's most expensive, best, and most spoiled soccer player, right before the World Cup finals. But of course he couldn't afford Ibranaldovez. Sure, Rublov was the richest man in the world, richer than Billion Gates, Michael Bloombucks, and Wampum Buffett combined. And Rublov did own Finland, New Zealand, eighteen factories puffing out thick smoke and skinny child laborers, twenty-four politicians, Chelchester Stadium, four taxicab permits, and a stolen bike with twenty-four gears. But that didn't help, because everyone knew that *no one* had enough money to buy Ibranaldovez. The last people to try had offered nineteen hundred million pounds sterling, a silver spoon, Tajikistan, three aircraft carriers, a freshly washed skyscraper, and two gently used propeller planes. When they got a *no*, they upped their offer to include the Dominican Republic, a stretch of prime real estate in downtown Oslo, three fat traveler's checks, and Queen Maud Land. Without even asking Queen Maud first. And they still got a resounding "No!"

"Your Highness," said the servant in the doorway. "The governor of the central bank is here, and——"

"Send him in," the king of Norway said, without looking up from the screen.

"Isn't it terrible?" the bank governor gasped, storming into the room.

"Yeah," said the king. "Can you believe it? All that money."

"So you've already heard?" the bank governor asked, startled, staring at the king in amazement.

"Of course. It's on TV right now," the king said. "Rublov doesn't even need to buy Ibranaldovez to beat Rotten Ham. After all, they're just a cut-rate soccer team from the dregs at the bottom of the fourth division."

"No, I'm talking about the robbery!" Bank Governor Tor said.

"What robbery?" the king asked.

"Someone made off with our entire gold reserve last night!"

"What are you talking about, Tor? Someone stole our entire gold— But wait, we only had the *one* gold bar, right? Aren't we insured against theft?"

"Well, yes, but—"

"The deductible's not too high, I hope?" the king asked.

"No, but—"

"Then I think you ought to be reporting this to the police instead of bothering me in the middle of the sports news," the king scolded.

"No, no, we can't do that. It'll cause panic," the bank governor said.

"What kind of panic?"

"A financial panic," the bank governor said.

"Hmm," the king said, thoughtfully resting an index finger against his chin. "I do believe I was out sick with a cold the day we covered economics in king school."

"I see," the bank governor said. "So, it's like this. People have to believe that they can exchange all the paper bills we print for actual gold that we have in the Bank of Norway's vault. If they find out that we don't have any gold there, everyone will panic. There will be a run on the bank, with everyone trying to cash in their bills for gold, and—*swoosh!*—all of a sudden Norwegian currency will be worthless, and we'll be dirt poor."

"That wouldn't be *so* bad, would it?" the king said. "How poor are we talking?"

"What do you mean, Your Highness?"

"Well, being as poor as Sweden wouldn't be so bad," the king said. "We're not talking about being as poor as East Austria, are we?"

"East Austria?" the bank governor asked.

"Sure. Of course things are going great in West Austria, but I hear that in the hardest-hit parts of

East Austria, there are a lot of families who can't afford a second car or a vacation home in the mountains. And a lot of people have to work at least eight hours a day just to be able to afford to vacation in Thailand."

"I'm afraid we're talking even poorer than that, Your Highness," the bank governor said.

"What? Give me an idea of exactly how poor."

Frustrated, the bank governor contemplated various ways of explaining the delicate economic situation to the king, but they all required some mention of, well, economics and were therefore pointless. Then he glanced up at the sports news and had a flash of inspiration. There was a soccer team, the team from North Central London, an area with one of the UK's highest unemployment and poverty rates. Surely that would convey the seriousness of the situation to the king. Bank Governor Tor cleared his throat and said, "Um . . . Rotten Ham poor?"

"Good God, man!" The king flung his blanket aside, leaped out of bed, and stuck his feet into his sable slippers. "Immediate action! Call the army! Raise interest rates! Enact a curfew! What can we do?"

"We could . . . uh, find the gold bar. We have until next Monday. That's when the World Bank is coming to do their annual inspection. If the gold bar isn't in the vault then, the news will get out and we'll be done for."

The king marched over to the door, opened it, and yelled, "Call up the secret service!"

"Do we have a secret service?" the bank governor cautiously asked from behind the king.

"Unfortunately, I'm not at liberty to answer that, Tor," the king said, walking over to the window and looking out over Oslo. He determined that people were walking around as usual on the streets below, and that it didn't seem like anyone knew anything yet. "If we have secret service, I would call them in and you would explain the situation to them. Understood? Good Lord, as poor as the Rotten Ham soccer team and the entire nation of East Austria . . ."

AT SIX MINUTES to eleven that morning, two men were standing stiffly at attention in the king's office. They were both dressed in long gray coats with sinister-looking, upturned collars and dark sunglasses, which made them look extremely secretive. So secretive that if you'd seen them on the street, you probably would have thought, *Hmm, these two look like the kind of people you could safely ask to do something secret.* Perhaps because you could see a little bit of the white stripes on the sides of their trouser legs where they stuck out under their coats, but especially because they were both wearing the black hats with the big, lopsided, floppy ostrich-feather tassels of the Norwegian Royal Guard. Which of course could mean only one thing: They must be in the Royal Guard's secret service.

"You can stop standing at attention," Bank Governor Tor said. "The king won't be here until he finishes his breakfast."

The two guardsmen immediately relaxed and started tugging on their mustaches.

"I assume you guys are with the Royal Guard's secret service," Tor said.

"And just what makes you say that?" the one with the handlebar mustache said, scowling with suspicion.

"Because of your hats with the floppy horse-tail thingies . . . uh, sorry, tassels."

"I think we'd better keep an extra-close eye on this wise guy here. Don't you, Helge?" Mr. Handlebar said.

"I think you're right, Hallgeir," said the other one, tugging on his Fu Manchu mustache. "Besides, it's not called the Royal Guard's secret service anymore," Mr. Fu Manchu continued. "Some tagger changed the sign to read the Secret Gourd. Then the organic farming activists painted a big gourd on there. . . . Sorry, where was I? Well, anyway, we had a secret meeting and decided to keep those changes. They could only help with the secrecy, right? So let me just put it this way: *If* the secret service did exist, it would be called the Secret Gourd."

"Exactly," said Mr. Handlebar. "But that's a secret, so don't tell anyone. And remember that we haven't said a single word about the fact that we're in the Secret Gourd. Have we, Helge?"

"Not a single word that I've heard, Hallgeir," Fu Manchu answered. "Because that's the first rule of the Secret Gourd. We don't say a word about our working there. Whoops, allow me to make a correction: *They* don't say a single word about *their* working there. But that's secret too. Got it?"

"Got it, Helge."

"I wasn't talking to you, Hallgeir. I was talking to the civilian."

"Got it," said Bank Governor Tor. "So, have you two heard what happened?"

"It's a secret," Helge said. "Both the thing that happened, and whether we know about it."

Just then the door opened and the king came in. Helge and Hallgeir snapped to attention.

"Good morning, guardsmen, ahem, gourdsmen," the king said.

"Good morning, Your Royal Highness. We hope your breakfast was good."

"It was just poached eggs with smashed saddle of pheasant on freshly baked, lightly toasted whole-grain bread. But I'm full, I've brushed my teeth, and I'm ready to see about who can help us find the gold."

Mr. Handlebar turned off the lights in the room, and Mr. Fu Manchu turned on the slide projector. A picture of a tall man with a long scar on his face appeared on the wall.

"First of all, there's this guy," Mr. Fu Manchu said. "His name is Harry, and he would probably be our first choice as investigator. Unfortunately, he's abroad right now."

"They say he's in Hong Kong, smoking bad things. An ugly habit, Your Highness," Mr. Handlebar said.

"Yes, to be sure. Then there's this woman," Mr. Fu

Manchu continued. The picture on the wall showed a thin reed of a woman with black hair. She had a roller skate on one foot. "Her name's Raspa, and apparently she can travel through time. We thought maybe she could go back to the day before the robbery and just move the gold bar to a safer place."

"Unfortunately, no one's seen her for ages. Some people say she disappeared back around the time of the French Revolution," Mr. Handlebar said.

"And then there's this guy," Mr. Fu Manchu continued, showing the next slide. The picture on the wall was blurry. It showed a tall building with something green in front of it. "This photo was taken by an amateur, but this is the only known photo of a man who supposedly has superpowers. He can turn into a human frog that can jump thirty feet straight up and stick his tongue out at least that far. We thought he might be able to snatch the gold back with his tongue. Unfortunately, we don't know where or who he is."

"But of course we'll track down whichever Your Highness might like us to," Mr. Handlebar concluded.

Silence.

"Um, Your Highness?" Mr. Fu Manchu asked.

They heard faint snoring. Mr. Handlebar flipped on the lights.

The king woke with a start, spluttering, "Who am I? Where am I? Not in Austria, right?! Please, not in Eastern—"

"Which of them would you like to save Norway, Your Highness?"

"Save Norway, yes!" the king said, raising his index finger. "There is only one person in this country who can save Norway."

"Only one, Your Highness?"

The king raised two more fingers. "Or three. Actually, there are three. And you need to get hold of them today."

"And what's so special about these three that makes Your Highness think they can save Norway?"

"Because these three saved the world from that big moon invasion."

"Uh, I'm sorry . . . what invasion?"

"You don't remember it, because you were hypnotized like all the rest of Norway. It's a long story, but it happened, believe me. I was with them, and they saved the world," the king said.

"Who are they? Secret superagents? Superheroes with top-notch training? The Norwegian men's curling team?"

The king got up from his chair, strode over to the window, and rocked back and forth on his heels as he looked out over his capital city for the second time. People were still acting totally normal. But it wouldn't last, not if they found out about the gold robbery. Which they were sure to do next week when the World Bank came for the inspection. East Austria, yikes!

"Doctor Victor Proctor," the king said. "And Lisa and Nilly."

The Big Recruitment

IT WAS EXACTLY sixteen minutes past three in the afternoon when Hallgeir (the secret gourdsman with the handlebar mustache) and Helge (the just-as-secret gourdsman with the Fu Manchu mustache) rang the doorbell at the little red house on Cannon Avenue in Oslo. The birds were singing and everything seemed peaceful. Well, everything *was* peaceful.

A man with a big paunch opened the door and bellowed in a friendly, authoritative voice, "Well, what do you know? The Secret Gourd came to see us! What can I do for you boys?"

"How did you know we—" Mr. Handlebar spluttered, chewing on the tips of his mustache in irritation.

"Forget about it, Helge," Hallgeir said. "Commandant, is your daughter at home?"

"Lisa? She's—"

Just then a frightful, piercing scream was heard from somewhere inside the house.

"That's her!" Mr. Handlebar yelled, pushing the Commandant aside. "Someone beat us to it! We have to rescue her!"

The two Secret Gourds stormed into the house and up the stairs to where the terrible, pained sound was coming from. They yanked open the door to what turned out to be a girl's bedroom and stood there staring in shock. Then they flung their hands up to cover their ears.

A girl was sitting on a chair in the middle of the room. She didn't look like a superagent, more like a very ordinary girl with brown braids, a few freckles, and friendly blue eyes that were looking up at the two Gourds in astonishment. There was a music stand in front of her, and there was something tubular and black hanging out of her mouth, making horrendous sounds.

"What—what's going on?!" Hallgeir yelled.

The girl took the tubular thing out of her mouth.

"What do you mean *what's going on?*" Lisa said. "I'm practicing my clarinet. The Dølgen School Marching Band is going to play 'God Save the Queen' tomorrow at the PTA meeting. What do you guys want?"

"Uh," Hallgeir said. "If you're Lisa, then Norway needs your help."

"It does?" Lisa said, surprised.

"Well, um," said Helge, looking skeptically around

the completely normal-looking girl's bedroom with posters of some pop stars on the walls, a globe, and a couple of stuffed animals that looked even less super-heroesque than the girl. "Someone thinks so, yes."

IT WAS EXACTLY twenty-one minutes past three when Hallgeir and Helge waded into the tall grass in front of the crooked blue house that stood all by itself at the very end of Cannon Avenue. They followed the dull banging coming from the back of the house, and when they rounded the corner, they met a strange sight. A withered man with bushy hair, wearing a doctor's lab coat and something that looked like swim goggles, was standing underneath a pear tree in the middle of the yard. He was balancing on one leg. He was painstakingly lifting his other leg—shod in something that looked like an old, hand-stitched black leather ankle boot— over a chopping block with a piece of firewood on it. Then he dropped his foot. There was a thump as the

heel of the boot slammed down on the piece of wood, which split into two. Each piece of firewood fell off opposite sides of the chopping block. The tall, skinny man kicked first one piece and then the other. They both sailed through the air, across the yard, and over to the wall of the house, where they landed neatly on a pile of stacked wood.

"Doctor Proctor, I presume?"

The skinny man straightened his back and beamed at Helge and Hallgeir. "Did you see that? Bang, bam, chopped and stacked right onto the woodpile! I'm working on a model that'll take down full trees. Just think what that will do for the lumber industry. Wait, is that why you guys are here?" The strange man brightened up even more. "Yes! You must have read the letter I sent to the minister of timber and lumberjacking affairs! You're here to buy my invention! I'm out of debt!"

"Um, not exactly, sir," said Hallgeir, straightening his tasseled hat. "We're here to—"

"Wait, let me guess!" Doctor Proctor said. "You're from the patent office, and you came to see the new aiming mitten I just submitted a patent application for?"

"No, we're—"

"Then you must be from the national dart-throwing team. But you know it would be cheating to use the mitten."

"Professor," Helge said. "We're here to ask you to save Norway as we know it."

AT EXACTLY QUARTER to four the representatives of the Secret Gourd were standing outside the little yellow house on Cannon Avenue, ringing the doorbell. A girl in her teens opened the door.

"Is Nilly here?" Helge asked.

"Who's Nilly?" the girl responded.

Helge cleared his throat and rocked on his heels. "The Nilly that they claim supposedly saved the world from being invaded by creatures from the moon, my dear?"

"I am not your *dear*, you weirdo. And my brother, that little squirt, is gone!" the girl said, staring at them with open hostility. "Are you guys from *Norway's Biggest Liar*?"

"Norway's what? What are you implying?" Hallgeir asked, peering over the top of his sunglasses.

"Are you back to do another mock interview with us?" the girl asked.

"A mock interview about what?" Hallgeir asked.

"About Nilly saving the world, of course. You know what happened after you tricked us into doing it last time? My mom cried for three days, and I couldn't show my face at school without being a laughingstock. 'That's the girl whose brother is a big liar,' and all that stuff." The girl was so mad the pimples on her red face were glowing. "So we decided to just pretend we've forgotten all about Nilly, you see?"

"I . . . uh, see," Hallgeir said. "But it's very important that we find him. Where did he go?"

"We don't know any Nilly, I'm telling you! And

besides, I promised Nilly—cross my heart—that I wouldn't tell anyone where he is, that numbskull."

"Cross your heart?"

"That little gnome paid me fifty kroner to cross my heart," she said, the corners of her mouth drooping down into an ugly grimace.

The Secret Gourds exchanged looks.

"What if we gave you a hundred?" Helge said tentatively.

"What do you take me for? He's my brother!"

"Oh, well then," Hallgeir said, and they turned around to leave.

"Wait!" the girl said.

They turned around again. "Yes?"

"Two hundred," she said, rolling her eyes and holding out her hand.

THE ELDERLY COUPLE stared at the tiny, eager, redheaded boy, who was so small he was barely visible behind the sales counter in the store they'd just walked into.

"No," the elderly man explained. "We don't want to buy a hang glider, we're just a little lost. I told you. So if you could please just tell us which way to go so we get out of this backwoods, godforsaken South Trøndelag place to somewhere where there are *people*."

"Not only will you receive a thirty percent discount and an extra set of tent poles so that you can also use the hang glider as a tent in the event that you're forced to land in the mountains," Nilly said, now hopping up and down on top of the counter, "you'll also receive a bag of charcoal!"

"Now you listen to me! My wife is afraid of heights, so we're never going to—" the man continued to protest.

"And that's not all!" Nilly yelled. "You'll also receive a map of South Trøndelag, western Sweden, and half of eastern Norway!"

"No, no, no! Which way to the highway, boy?" the man yelled.

"If you buy one, just one, little hang glider, I'll throw in a map that will show you how to get out of here and find your way to Gothenburg or northeastern Blåfjella-Skjækerfjella all by yourselves. And since it's such a beautiful day today, I've just decided to throw in one packet—no, not one, but *two* packets of hot cocoa mix! So, what do you say?"

"No!" the man bellowed, slamming his fist down on the counter so hard that his anxious, acrophobic wife shuddered, causing her hat to slide to one side, where it hung at a funny angle.

Nilly nodded. "I can see that you need a little time to consider my offer, my good man. Well, well, then it would be a pleasure for me to explain to you how to get out of here. It shouldn't be that hard. As you can see, everyone else has already figured out how to do it. No one's here!"

Nilly continued, "I just wonder if I could be so bold as to ask you if you wouldn't mind dropping this postcard in the mail for me once you reach civilization. It's to my friends, Lisa and Doctor Proctor."

The woman nodded, pushed her hat back into place, and took the postcard while the boy spread out the map and started explaining to the man how to reach civilization. She read the postcard.

DEAR ~~█████████~~
FRIENDS!

EVERY DAY IS A PARTY HERE! PETTER AND I ARE ENJOYING OURSELVES TO THE BEST OF OUR ABILITIES! DRINKING HOT CHOCOLATE, ~~█████████~~ ~~█████████~~, PLAYING CHINESE CHECKERS, AND SELLING HANG GLIDERS TO BEAT THE BAND!

SINCERELY, NILLY

TO:
LISA AND
DR. PROCTOR
CANNON AVE
OSLO, NORWAY

THE KING

Nilly stood out in front of the store, waving as the old couple's car disappeared down the country road, kicking up a cloud of dust behind it. The sound of its engine faded away, and all that could be heard was cautious birdsong from the vast forests that surrounded the hangar, which bore a large banner that said SALE! HANG GLIDERS 30% OFF WHILE SUPPLIES LAST!!!

But as Nilly stood there, he heard something else. A voice. It was coming from the air somewhere far above him.

"Heh-heh, Nilly! NILLY! Look!"

Nilly put his hand up to block the sun and peered up at the hang glider circling in the air above him. A person wearing a snug-fitting red bodysuit, which was extra tight over his potbelly, and a pair of glasses with lenses so thick they looked like big marbles, dangled underneath the glider.

"Look at me! I'm Petter! I'm the one and only Petter! New record, Nilly! I flew almost to Denmark and back!

Hurray for Petter!" the man in the red bodysuit—who it appeared might be named Petter—sang and bragged, grinning down at Nilly, who was waving up at him frenetically.

"Great, Petter!" Nilly yelled back. "But watch out, don't you see the—"

There was a crunch and an ominous creaking from the frame and wings of the hang glider as it crashed into the wall of the store, snapping the TV antenna and then tumbling to the ground.

Nilly ran over to Petter, who was already standing up amid the wreckage, brushing gravel and grass off his potbelly.

"Yikes, Petter, you've got to look where you're going!" Nilly said.

"Why bother? It's not like I can see anything anyway," Petter said, breathing on his thick glasses and then rubbing them on his bodysuit. "I flew all the way to the coast, Nilly! Soon I'll make it all the way to Denmark. Then I can buy us some Danishes to go with our hot chocolate. Hmm, now that I mention hot chocolate . . ."

"I'll go reheat the batch we made this morning," Nilly said with a sigh.

Half an hour later they were sitting in the kitchen, each drinking from their mug as Petter stared at the Chinese checkers board in deep concentration.

"I've been thinking," Petter said.

"Yes," Nilly said. "You've been thinking for more than twenty minutes, and you haven't even moved your first marble yet. Maybe it's about time you—"

"I wasn't talking about the Chinese checkers," Petter said. "I was thinking that you've been up here for a long time now. Not that I'm not enjoying having you around, but . . ."

"I can't go back home, Petter. Oh, the humiliation, the humiliation! My whole school, my whole family, they're all laughing at me. All my friends . . ."

"All of them? How many friends do you—" Petter began.

"Well, okay, fine. Both of them . . . They warned me, said I should bite my tongue, not talk about how we saved the world from invisible baboon monsters from the moon. They said no one would believe us anyway, but like the idiot I am, I—"

"Don't be so hard on yourself, Nilly! You're not an idiot!" Petter protested.

"Yes, I am!"

"No, no. You're way smarter than . . . than me, for example," Petter said.

"No, I'm not."

"Yes, you definitely are, Nilly!"

"No."

"Yes!"

"Okay, fine, so I am," Nilly said, slurping his cocoa.

"Shh," said Petter, looking up. "What's that sound?"

"Um, hello? It's called slurping," Nilly said.

"No, not that sound, *that* sound!" Petter said, pointing to the ceiling.

Nilly listened and sure enough, there was a *floppety-floppety-flop* sound that was getting louder.

Nilly peered out the kitchen window. A sudden gust of wind caused the pine trees to sway, dust to kick up from the country road, and the grass to lie down. The sound just got louder and louder, and a shadow settled over the lawn.

And as Nilly and Petter sat drinking their hot chocolate, a vehicle suspended in thin air slowly touched down, stopping right outside the kitchen window as tufts of grass, chickens, and pinecones all blew away.

"What do you suppose that is?" Petter said, taking a sip of his cocoa.

"Looks like a helicopter," Nilly said.

The banner saying SALE! HANG GLIDERS 30% OFF WHILE SUPPLIES LAST!!! came loose and blew away.

"I can see that, but who are those guys inside it?"

"Based on their sunglasses and hats, I'd say they're from the secret service."

"Well, well, I guess we'd better make some more cocoa, then."

Nilly Makes a Decision

"NO," NILLY SAID.

"No what?" said Hallgeir, adjusting his hat. He slurped his hot chocolate and looked around at the kitchen.

"No, I don't want to take the assignment," Nilly said.

"Why not?" asked Helge, wiping hot chocolate off

his mustache. "The king is personally asking you to save Norway from financial ruin!"

"Thanks, but I already saved Norway one time, and look at what happened," Nilly said.

"But . . . they stole the national gold reserves. Our people need you, Nilly!" Helge pleaded.

"Do they?" Nilly asked. "To laugh at, maybe."

"Laugh? What do you mean?" Hallgeir said.

"Go home, my good men," Nilly said, crossing his arms. "Go home and tell the king and the people of Norway that even though they've stolen my unusually good name and sullied my reputation, I still have my pride." Nilly's voice quavered slightly. "Tell them this time they're on their own, no Nilly is going to save them this time. Norway is on its own! I'm heading for the hills!"

And with that Nilly stood up and marched out. Hallgeir and Helge looked at each other in confusion. And then they looked at Petter.

"I guess you guys haven't seen it," said Petter.

"Seen what?" Helge asked.

"Is it something secret?" Hallgeir asked eagerly, sounding excited.

"No, it's something on YouTube," Petter said.

"We only look at secret things," Hallgeir said. "PBS and stuff like that."

"It was on TV, too," Petter said. "*Norway's Biggest Liar.*"

"Oh, right. Nilly's sister mentioned that show," Helge said.

Two minutes later Petter had the computer on and was playing the YouTube clip. It showed a reporter standing on Cannon Avenue in front of the yellow house that Helge and Hallgeir had just been to a few hours earlier. The reporter whispered, grinning at the camera, "On today's episode of *Norway's Biggest Liar*, we're visiting the Oslo home of the person rumored to be the biggest—and probably also the smallest—liar in all of Norway. As usual, we will be pretending that we're a serious show and that we believe *everything* he says. Come on, let's go in and meet his mother and sister. . . ."

The next scene showed two people on a sofa in a messy living room. One of them was the girl Helge and Hallgeir had spoken to at Nilly's house; the other was a woman in a pink quilted bathrobe.

"Nilly started out by just exaggerating a little," the woman said, looking somberly into the camera. "Gradually the exaggerations got bigger and bigger. Ultimately he claimed that he and his friends had saved the world and traveled through time in a bathtub."

"Where do you think he got this compulsion to lie?" the reporter asked.

"Not from me, at any rate. I'm sure it's from his father's side. His grandfather wrote a book called *Animals You Wish Didn't Exist*. Solid lies from beginning to end," Nilly's mother told the reporter.

"From end to beginning," Nilly's sister added snidely.

The next scene showed Nilly on his way into a talk show studio, victoriously raising both arms as the audience cheered wildly for him.

"He has no idea they're making fun of him," Petter said with a sigh.

"Welcome to the set of *Norway's Biggest* (cough!)*ar*," said the reporter, now wearing a nice suit. "Is it really true that you traveled back in time to the Battle of Waterloo?"

"Of course," Nilly replied.

The audience responded by applauding, and Nilly turned to face them and bowed politely.

"So I suppose you met Napoléon, too, huh?" the reporter asked.

"Of course," Nilly said with a patient smile, and then clasped his hands and put his fingertips together. "Yes, for a while I actually *was* Napoléon. That's how I managed to prevent the battle."

"So you *were* Napoléon and you *stopped* the Battle of Waterloo and kept it from happening?" the reporter said.

"Someone had to do it, and I happened to be there," Nilly said as modestly as he could, studying his own well-nibbled fingernails.

Wild cheers from the audience. Meanwhile close-ups showed that they were laughing so hard they were practically falling out of their seats.

"And with that, a round of applause to thank

Nilly, aka Napoléon!" the reporter exclaimed.

Thunderous applause as an attractive woman escorted a waving, smiling Nilly offstage.

Once Nilly was out of camera and hearing range, the reporter turned to face the camera and whispered, "I think we've got a strong contender here for the title of Norway's Biggest Liar. But the ultimate decision is up to you, viewers. When you cast your votes . . ."

Petter turned off the computer.

"Not so surprising that he's had enough and doesn't want to do it again," Helge said.

"How are we going to convince him?" Hallgeir asked.

"We need to talk about fighting for home and family and king and fatherland," Helge said.

"Yeah, and for keeping our Norwegian currency!" Hallgeir said.

"Good thinking, Hallgeir! And then we can play

touching music in the background while we say all this, and as the music swells we'll talk louder and louder and get choked up," Helge said.

"Good thinking, Helge. Let's go find that little pipsqueak and—" Hallgeir began.

But just then there was a loud, complaining creak from the hinges as someone yanked the door open. And a second later it banged loudly as someone slammed it shut again. Nilly stood before them with a backpack on his back.

"We thought you'd headed for the hills," Hallgeir said.

"I changed my mind," Nilly said.

"Put on the touching music," Helge whispered hurriedly to Petter. "I'll start talking about home and the fatherland and—"

"If you guys are done with your hot chocolate, I'm ready to head back to Oslo now," Nilly said.

"What? But I haven't even gotten to the part where

I get all choked up yet . . . ," Hallgeir began.

"No need. As I said, I changed my mind," Nilly explained.

"Really?" Helge asked.

Nilly shrugged and picked at his front teeth with a dirty fingernail. "Really. Hang gliders and Chinese checkers are nice and all, but a gold heist sounds way more exciting. And a guy can only drink *so* many cups of hot chocolate, right?"

And so it came to be that exactly thirty-three minutes and twenty-four seconds after six thirty, Zulu time, *floppety-floppety-flop* sounds were once again heard over this remote village, now almost completely devoid of inhabitants. Petter stood on the hill and waved good-bye to them.

Nilly sat next to the pilot, wearing ear protectors that practically covered his entire teeny tiny redheaded head with the freckles and the turned-up nose. He was begging and pleading for a chance to fly the helicopter, just for a little bit. He swore—*cross my heart!*—that he'd flown bombers during both world wars, not to mention that he had been the first person under the age of eighteen to fly an unmanned rocket to Saturn and those parts.

Our Friends Learn Everything About the Mission. Well, Not Quite EVERYTHING...

THE KING TUGGED at his annoyingly tight royal sash, cleared his throat, and pushed back his IKEA desk chair. He'd tried moving his throne into his office, but the seat was so high that it ended up squishing his thighs between the seat and the desk. In front of him stood the only people in the kingdom who knew that Norway's gold reserves had been stolen: Hallgeir and Helge of the Secret Gourd; Tor, the governor of the Bank of Norway; Doctor Proctor, Lisa, and Nilly.

"The gold needs to be back in the Bank of Norway's vault by next Monday when the World Bank does its inspection," the king said. "If it's not, we'll be bankrupt and forced to live like the East Austrians. Is that what we want? Yes or no?"

"Uh . . . ," Lisa said, looking at Doctor Proctor, who was raising one eyebrow, and Nilly, who was squinting one eye shut as he thoughtfully scratched his sideburn.

"Can we have more options?" Nilly asked.

"The correct answer is no!" the king bellowed. "Norway is counting on the three of you now. The good news is that the Secret Gourd's thorough investigation has procured some information for us, which means you will not be starting out with absolutely nothing."

"The experts checked the hole in the bank vault," Hallgeir said. "The robbers must have used a drill with a diamond-tipped bit with a really humongous diamond on it. The only diamond in the world big enough was recently stolen from Johannesburg, South Africa."

"Also, we recently talked to our colleagues in the Brazilian secret service," Helge said. "This is a secret, but last week the central bank of Brazil's gold reserves were also stolen. The Brazilian authorities haven't said anything about it, because they're afraid of becoming just as poor as the Argentinians."

"And clever as we are, we cross-checked the passenger lists of people who've flown between Johannesburg, Oslo, and Brazil in recent weeks. And it's not that long a list. Nothing like the traffic jam of Norwegians trying to drive across the border into Strömstad, Sweden, to stock up on liquor, where the taxes are lower."

"Or Kragerø, the Cape Cod of Norway," Helge said.

"Or Ål in Hallingdal, famous for its, uh, cross-country skiing," Hallgeir said.

"Get to the point," said the king.

"And," Helge continued, "there are only three people who have been to all three of those locations recently. And these three are not just anyone."

"Quite the contrary," Hallgeir said. "They are specifically *them*."

"The point!" the king yelled. "Get to it!"

"Wouldn't you know, they traveled under assumed names, claiming to be the Brunch Brothers, but they didn't fool us, no they did not, no sirree. The three are actually"—Helge paused, looking around at all the curious faces to make sure everyone was holding their breath—"the Crunch Brothers!" Helge looked around triumphantly, but the faces around him were not those of people gasping in shock or even looking very scared.

"The Crunch Brothers are known as the most awful

bandits in all of Great and Small Britain combined," Hallgeir explained.

"Cool!" shouted Nilly. "Awful bandits are cool!"

"What I'm wondering," Doctor Proctor said, "is how these brothers managed to take Norway's *entire* gold reserves with them on a plane. I mean, when you consider how heavy gold is, well, they must have paid a fortune for overweight baggage."

"It was only one gold bar," Bank Governor Tor said with a small, modest smile. "So, definitely under the weight limit."

"Only one gold bar?" Lisa said, raising an incredulous eyebrow. "That's Norway's entire gold reserve?"

"It's shrunk a little over the years," Tor admitted.

"I'd say," said Proctor. "What happened to the rest of the gold?"

"Candy," Tor said with a casual shrug.

"The gold turned into *candy*?" Nilly asked.

"No, into gold fillings for cavities," Tor said. "After

World War Two, Norwegians started eating so much candy that by the 1970s, dentists ran out of gold. Maybe you remember 1972, the year of the Great Toothache?"

Everyone else shook their heads. Only the king nodded, his hand flying instinctively up to his jaw.

"That was an ugly time," Tor said. "You could hear the moaning and groaning and cries of pain from North Cape, at the northernmost tip of Norway, all the way south to Lindesnes at the southernmost tip. And boy could you hear them! The Parliament had to pass the Dental Transference Act. And every year since then, the dentists of Norway have been steadily eating away at the central bank's gold reserves. Until today . . ."

"So all our gold is in the mouths of candy-eating Norwegians who didn't brush their teeth?" Lisa asked, crossing her arms and looking offended. "That's just not right!"

"Yup," Nilly said, plunging his index fingers into the corners of his mouth and pulling it open so far it looked like the top half of his head might fall off. "Ust looooookh at dis. . . ."

And sure enough: His mouth gleamed with the dull sheen of unbrushed gold.

"But if you *know* these Crunch Brother people are behind the robberies, why haven't you already arrested them?" Doctor Proctor asked.

"There are several reasons," Bank Governor Tor said. "First of all, we don't have any actual evidence, just the plane tickets."

"Well, but they must have hidden the gold somewhere," Lisa said. "All we have to do is ransack their garage, basement, and—"

"Attic!" Nilly yelled. "Brazilian gold in the attic! Cool!"

"I'm sure the Crunch Brothers probably handed the gold over ages ago to whoever masterminded this. There's no way the brothers are smart enough to have come up with such clever robberies themselves. The question is, who masterminded all this?" the bank governor said, shaking his head.

"The police could just arrest the Crunch Brothers and get them to say who they gave the gold to, right?" Lisa said.

The bank governor sighed. "If only it were so easy, Lisa. But these are hardened criminals. They're not going to blab, no matter how much you torture them. Not that anyone is going to be tortured, of course . . ."

"Torture! Torture!" Nilly cheered, hopping up and down. "Torture! Just a little?"

"Unfortunately, the UN has decided that even gentle torture is illegal," the king said with a sigh, tugging at his tight sash. "So the only way for us to find the gold is to infiltrate this gang. In other words, we have to pretend we're one of them, make friends with them, gain their trust. And then we can trick them—maybe over a beer at the pub when they feel like bragging a little bit—into telling us where the gold is."

"Why don't you just get a police agent in England to do that?" Lisa asked. "I mean, they already speak English and everything, right?"

"We talked to the police agents, as you call them," Helge said.

"Or Scotland Yard, as *we* call them," Hallgeir said, with a snooty look on his face.

"And they said the Crunch Brothers would spot a real police officer a mile away. They can smell if you're with the police," Helge said.

"That's true. Police officers smell like stuffed cabbage rolls," Hallgeir said.

"So Scotland Yard thought it would be a good idea to trick the brothers using kids or crazy professors, because then they definitely wouldn't smell anything," Helge said.

"So, do you understand your mission?" the king asked.

"Yes sir, sire, sir!" Nilly said, snapping to attention

and saluting. "And if a *tiny little bit* of torture should end up being necessary, do we have permission for that? How about noogies? Wedgies? Wet willies? General tickling?"

"You're heading to London early tomorrow morning," the king said. "You'll be meeting a secret Scotland Yard informant by the Michael Jackson figure in Madame Tourette's Wax Museum at exactly eight minutes past one. The informant has more information for you about the Crunch Brothers. And remember, this is a secret mission, so if you end up being captured . . ."

"No one's going to come rescue us!" Nilly cheered. "I LOVE it! I just love it."

Lisa rolled her eyes, and Doctor Proctor gave Nilly a serious, concerned look.

"Any questions?" the king asked.

"Do the brothers have any particular distinguishing characteristics that might make it easier for us to recognize them?" Doctor Proctor asked.

The king looked at the guards, who looked at each other, shrugged, and then shook their heads.

"Nothing?" Lisa asked.

"Not that we can think of," Hallgeir said. "Although, now that you mention it, I guess they do each have their first initial tattooed on their foreheads."

"But we don't know what letters those are, so I don't suppose that'll be much help," Helge said.

WITH A BIG smile, the king shook the hands of each of our heroes in turn and wished them good luck. After the three of them had left, however, he moved over to stand by the window. His smile was gone.

"I have the feeling that you're not telling me the whole truth about these Crunch Brothers," the king said.

"Oh?" Helge said innocently. "What do you mean by that?"

"I've never noticed police officers to smell of cabbage

rolls. I think you were lying," the king said. "So, were you?"

Helge cleared his throat. "Uh, yeah, we might have lied."

"But just a little," Hallgeir added.

"We didn't want to scare those two kids by telling them that no one at Scotland Yard dares to get close to the Crunch Brothers. Or worse yet, close to . . ." Helge lowered his voice and whispered something.

"What?" the king asked.

Helge whispered again.

"What did he say?" the king asked Hallgeir.

"He said . . ." Then Hallgeir lowered his voice and whispered something.

"Enough of this nonsense!" the king roared. "Who doesn't Scotland Yard dare to get close to?"

Helge walked all the way over to the king and whispered "Mama" into his ear.

Hallgeir walked over and whispered "Crunch" into the king's other ear.

"Mama?" the king asked. "Crunch?"

"Shh!" Helge said, looking around cautiously.

"Double shh!" Hallgeir said.

"She's the Crunch Brothers' mother," Helge whispered. "She's known as the worst thing to have happened to London since the Great Plague of 1665."

"She sees and hears everything, is impossible to trick, and is so horrible that no one will say her name out loud," Hallgeir whispered.

"Uh, pardon me for asking," the bank governor said. "But how horrible can three bank robbers and their mother actually be?"

"They play blood knuckles—you know, the card game—with anyone who tries anything," Hallgeir said, his eyes rolling halfway back in his head in fear.

The bank governor and the king gasped in unison.

"Blood knuckles?" they asked, looking in horror at the two Secret Gourds, who crossed their arms and nodded ominously.

"It's not really so serious if you only lose four or five rounds," Hallgeir said. "Then they just hit you on the knuckles a few times with the edge of the deck of cards and it stings a little and your knuckles get a little red."

"But if you lose ten thousand rounds . . . ," Helge said, rolling his eyes back in his skull so only the whites—and a little bit of red—showed.

"What happens then?" the bank governor asked.

"An agent from Scotland Yard once tried to infiltrate the family. Mama Crunch detected him, so they played bloody knuckles with him. He lost a big pot of ten thousand knuckle blows."

The Gourds shook their heads in unison.

"What happened?" the bank governor asked.

"Unfortunately, that information is rated NC-17," Hallgeir said.

"I assure you I'm well over seventeen," the king said with one eyebrow raised.

"Yes, but what about the people reading this right now?" Hallgeir asked.

"What?" the king said. "Reading what?"

"He didn't mean anything by that," Helge said, shooting Hallgeir a stern look. "You know that's a secret, Hallgeir!"

"Sorry, I forgot," Hallgeir said sheepishly.

The king puffed out his chest and roared, "This is a royal command: SPIT IT OUT!"

"They sliced the poor guy to bits with that deck of cards. He looked like a pile of shredded Parmesan when they were done with him."

The king and the bank governor stared speechlessly at the two Secret Gourd members.

"What—what have we gotten them into?" the king moaned.

"Oh, but I'm sure our three will do fine," Hallgeir said. "They probably won't get caught."

"No," said Helge. "I wouldn't think so, no."

The Art of Packing
for a Trip—to London,
for Example

"THERE'S AN ART to packing," Doctor Proctor said as he pulled a worn golf bag off a basement shelf. "What you *don't* bring is just as important as what you do bring. Let me hear about how you packed, my friends."

"I'm bringing this backpack," Lisa said, pointing to a red hiking backpack. "I've got toiletries, six changes of underwear, rain gear, a pocketknife, a pair of wool socks in case it gets cold, a first aid kit, a small flashlight, and a pair of extra good shoes in case we have to do a lot of walking."

"Aha!" said Doctor Proctor. "Spoken like a professional traveler who has traveled not only through space, but also through time! What about you, Nilly?"

"Even more professional!" Nilly said. He pointed

to a used plastic grocery bag, which he'd set down on the workbench next to a set of test tubes containing something ice blue, which was bubbling and smoking. "An almost fresh pair of underwear, nail polish remover, Monopoly in case it rains, and a bottle of malaria pills from my grandfather," Nilly said proudly.

"Malaria pills?" Doctor Proctor asked. "There aren't any malaria mosquitoes in London, Nilly."

"Ah, so they finally exterminated the London

Malaria Mosquito? Well, good, because truth be told, I wasn't sure about the expiration date on those pills. It says 3/12/25, but I wasn't sure if that was 2025. I think it might be 1925."

"What are you going to do with the nail polish remover?" Lisa asked. "You don't wear nail polish."

"Exactly," Nilly said. "So if I should happen to get some on me, I'd like to get it off as soon as possible."

"What about a toothbrush and more than one change of underwear?" Lisa said.

"My toothbrush is in my back pocket. I'll borrow toothpaste from you. And a professional traveler never wastes underwear. Besides, I'm an optimist."

"What do you mean?" Lisa asked.

"I figure we'll solve the case before I need to change my underwear more than once."

"Well, a good attitude is a good thing to take on a trip too," Doctor Proctor said. "What do you guys think I ought to bring along besides the usual necessities? Do you remember the language nose clips I invented so we could speak French? I've invented something even better now. It's a multilingual pill that makes it so we can speak and understand English for fourteen days. And they taste like raspberries!"

"Nilly definitely needs one of those," Lisa said. They were in the same English as a Foreign Language class in school.

"Hallo, jeg kan engelsk!" Nilly replied indignantly, in Norwegian. Then he corrected himself, saying, "I mean, I can English!" in some kind of Norwenglish.

Nilly stared at Lisa stiffly for a few seconds before he ultimately gave the tip of his freckled, upturned nose a slight, uncomfortable tug. "Okay, fine. *One* tiny little multilingual pill for me, then. Do you have any other new inventions, Doctor Proctor?"

"I have this wood-chopping shoe, which I made in your size, Nilly!" Doctor Proctor said.

"Yippee!" Nilly said, snatching the tiny shoe.

"I was planning to give it to you as a homecoming present, along with this," said Doctor Proctor, holding out an equally tiny mitten.

"What's that?" Nilly asked.

"What does it look like? Obviously, it's an aiming mitten for right-handed people," Doctor Proctor said.

"Oh, right, of course," Nilly said, and put it on.

"What's an . . . aiming mitten?" Lisa asked.

"Don't you even know that?" Nilly said, boxing at the air in front of him with the mitten.

"No," Lisa said. "What is it?"

"It's . . . a really nice mitten that keeps your right hand warm if your left hand isn't cold. And you can wear it for air-boxing to keep from getting a draft on your fingers, which would cause arthritis, so you'd have to hold the silverware with your left hand or your toes when you were eating in the old folks' home," Nilly explained.

"Well," Doctor Proctor said, smiling faintly. "First and foremost it's a mitten that you can throw these three darts with." He held up three small darts: one yellow, one orange, and one black. "And within a radius of ten meters, they'll hit within a millimeter of where you're aiming."

"Well, yeah, that too, of course," Nilly said, and kept air-boxing to make sure no one had any doubt the mitten was also particularly well suited to that. "Do you have anything else new?"

"Hmm," Doctor Proctor said, looking around. "In addition to an app that plays rock-scissors-paper, I did invent an antifreeze."

"Hasn't that already been invented?" Lisa asked.

"Not one like this," Doctor Proctor said, holding up one of the test tubes containing the bubbling, ice-blue substance. "If you drink this, it will react with the acid in your stomach and kidneys so that when you

pee, whatever you pee on will immediately freeze and turn into ice, which can be shattered. No matter what it's made of."

"No way!" Nilly exclaimed, clapping his hands with glee.

"As long as you don't pee on your own shoes," Lisa said dryly.

"I'll bring along a tiny bottle," Doctor Proctor said. "But then I guess that's it."

"You didn't invent anything for *me*?" Lisa asked.

The other two looked at her.

"Oh, you're right," Doctor Proctor said, looking slightly disappointed in himself. "I guess Nilly does always end up getting to test the inventions."

"That's not really such a bad thing," Lisa said, smiling bravely. "After all, he enjoys it more than I would."

"We could bring some fartonaut powder for Lisa," Nilly said. "And a big can of baked beans. Beans, beans, the magical fruit," Nilly sang. "The more you eat, the more you toot!"

"No!" Lisa said resolutely. "No beans, no farts. The peeing will be plenty."

"Just one packet," Nilly pleaded. "Just think, Lisa, once we've found the gold and we're celebrating with the queen at Buckingham Palace and you're all dressed up and have been dancing with some prince or other who's taking you on a romantic, moonlit tour of the gardens, then you can impress him by blowing all the leaves right out of the garden with a single fart."

"No, thank you!" Lisa said. "Forget I even asked!"

"But Lisa, the queen's gardener would beg us for the invention!" Nilly said. "Maybe Doctor Proctor could finally make some money off it."

"Well," said Doctor Proctor. "Since the Americans don't want to use the power to send their astronauts into space, I suppose we could bring one packet for the British. It's not like it takes much room."

"Jell-O!" Juliette Margarine, Doctor Proctor's girlfriend, called from the kitchen. Which was perfect timing, because they'd just finished packing.

"Now you guys be careful over there in London," Juliette said, her face showing her concern as she watched the three of them digging into the Jell-O. "And you promise you'll take good care of them."

"Yeah, yeah," Doctor Proctor said.

"I wasn't talking to you, Victor, I was talking to Lisa," Juliette said.

"Yeah, yeah," Lisa assured her with a smile.

"There's nothing to be afraid of," Nilly said, trying in vain to stifle a burp. "These Crunch people aren't even the worst in the world, just the worst in Great and Small Britain. And we're three of the cleverest people in all of Cannon Avenue."

They toasted to that with their favorite pear soda.

Afterward, Juliette gave each of them a hug, and they each went home: Nilly to the yellow house, Lisa to the red one, and Doctor Proctor down into the basement to do the last little bit of fine-tuning on the inventions he was going to bring.

When Nilly walked into the living room, his mother groaned. "You again?" without looking up from the TV.

"I'm happy to see you, too, Mom," Nilly said.

"Shh!" his sister Eva snarled. "*Total Makeover* is on."

"I'll be out of your hair tomorrow. I'm going to London," Nilly said, going into the kitchen to pour himself a glass of milk.

"Can you bring me two slices of bread with salami and a cup of tea, and three slices with Nutella for your sister?" his mother yelled. "And hurry it up, we're starving in here."

When Nilly came back with the requested items on a tray, his sister Eva handed him a freshly ironed two-hundred-kroner note.

"For me?" Nilly asked, lighting up.

"For you . . . to buy me something in London, you gnome! A cream called Clean Coocoo's."

"What kind of cream is it?"

"Zit cream."

"I thought you already had enough zits," Nilly said.

"*Anti*-zit cream then, you rutabaga brain! Just buy it, because if you don't, you're not getting your bedroom back. So there."

"My room?" Nilly asked.

"Oh yeah," his mother said with her mouth full of salami. "You were gone so long I couldn't stop her from taking over your room."

"But—but she already has her own," Nilly said, puzzled.

"So? Now she has two. So what?" his mother said. "A girl needs space for her clothes. But I'm sure she'll let you sleep there tonight. Right, Eva?"

"I guess," Eva sniffed. "But if you touch anything, we're going to sell you to a traveling circus."

"Keep your money and your zits!" Nilly said, crumpling up the two-hundred-kroner note and tossing it back to his sister. "I'm not buying you so much as an English tea bag!"

Eva put her hand over her mouth in horror. "Did you hear that, Mommy?! Did you hear what that freak just said to your only daughter?"

"Show your sister some respect, Nilly," his mother

mumbled, turning up the volume on the TV. "And make sure you do the dishes in the kitchen. As you can see, there's quite a backlog since you've been away so long."

Nilly went to the bedroom that was no longer his, pulled his toothbrush out of his plastic grocery store bag, brushed his teeth—the ones containing gold and the ones without—got undressed, and crawled into bed.

He lay there for a while with his eyes closed, imagining that he could hear the sounds his friends were making: Doctor Proctor hammering and drilling and boiling down there in his basement, Juliette snoring softly from their bedroom, and Lisa playing her clarinet from the other side of Cannon Avenue. But now she had finished practicing and had crawled into her bed as well.

So Nilly sat down in front of his window as usual and held his fingers up in front of his desk lamp so they cast shadows that turned into figures on his thin curtains. He was almost sure Lisa watched his shadow theater performances. And tonight's was about three friends who were pursuing three bandits and an entire little tiny country's gold reserve of one bar of gold. And before Lisa fell asleep, the three heroes got the bandits, the gold, half the kingdom, and at least two princesses.

Madame Tourette's Wax Museum and the King of Pop

IT WAS EXACTLY noon. It was a typical London day, and a typical London rain was falling over the city. And since it was exactly noon, Big Ben—which is a very precise and *biiiig* clock in a *biiiig* tower in the middle of London—started chiming. And as it struck the last of its typical twelve London clock chimes, the door of a hotel room at the Regent Courtyard Badger's Dingle Bottom Crossing opened.

"Look at this view," Lisa said, leaving the hotel room door open and racing over to the window. "We can see the Thames, Westminster Bridge, and Big Ben!"

"Dibs on the top bunk!" Nilly shouted, pushing Doctor Proctor aside.

"Ach, laddie, I dunna think they've got truckle beds," Doctor Proctor said in a funny accent. Nilly froze, staring dumbfounded at Doctor Proctor, who seemed to take no notice and continued, "There are beds for you and Lisa in the bedroom. I'll be sleepin' out here on the couch bed."

Nilly made a face and spluttered, "Couch bed? Truckle beds? What on earth are you talking about?"

Doctor Proctor sighed and set his golf bag down on the sofa. "Ach, I only had two language pills for the Queen's English. So I let you have them. I took the one for—"

"Scottish," Nilly said. "But still: truckle bed?"

"Scots English is a wee bit different, Nilly, but I'm sure you'll be able to ken me."

"Well, as long as you don't start wearing a kilt and playing the bagpipes," Nilly said, darting into the bed-room.

"Hey, you guys," Lisa said. "We've got to get over to Madame Tourette's Wax Museum. There might be a line to get in, and we have to be on time."

"Nag, nag, nag," Nilly called from the bedroom, where he'd spent a little time jumping on one of the beds before moving over to the other one and doing a little jumping there, too. "This one is sproingier," he announced. "Is it okay if I take the bed by the window, Lisa?"

"Yeah, sure. But what would you have done if I said no?" Lisa said with a sigh.

"Then obviously you could have had the bed by the wall," Nilly said. "I'm not unreasonable. Hey, I can touch the ceiling!"

"Come on!" Lisa urged.

"I just have to change," Nilly said.

"Nilly! If we want to make it there——"

"I'm ready!"

Lisa and Doctor Proctor stared. Nilly was standing in the doorway wearing a tweed jacket and a tweed deerstalker cap, which looked at least as ridiculous as the Secret Gourd horsetail-duster hats.

"What's wrong?" Nilly said. "Real detectives need disguises and secret code names, right? So from now on you guys can call me Sherl." Nilly stuck a curved pipe into his mouth. "And Lisa, you can be Ockolmes. And Doctor, you can be . . ."

"Doctor Mitten?" Lisa suggested.

Nilly scratched his sideburn. "No, it has to be something Scottish. Doctor MacKaroni."

"Macaroni?" Lisa said. "Isn't that Italian?"

"Yeah, about as Italian as MacElangelo or MacO'Polo," Nilly said. "And it tastes a lot better."

"Are you guys ready, Sherl? Ockolmes?" Doctor MacKaroni asked. "Because we've got to go now."

SURE ENOUGH, THERE was a line of tourists waiting to get into Madame Tourette's.

After they bought their tickets, our three friends entered the wax museum. They elbowed their way through the crowd of people and life-sized wax celebrities, with Doctor Proctor pointing out Elvis, Marilyn Monroe, John F. Kennedy, and Winston Churchill.

"Hey, I was that guy once!" Nilly said, pointing to a short figure in a uniform and tricorne hat.

"That's right, it's Napoléon," Doctor Proctor said.

"Ugh," Lisa said with a shudder. "It's impossible to tell who's alive and who's made of wax in here."

"Oh, look over there!" Nilly said, pointing. "It's Ibranaldovez!"

They stopped in front of a wax figurine in a soccer uniform.

"Are you sure?" Lisa asked. "The face doesn't look that much like Ibranaldovez."

"No, but *that* looks a lot like him," Nilly said, pointing to the wax figure's hand, whose fingers were all clenched into a fist except for the middle one, which was sticking straight up.

"Here's the Michael Jackson figure," Doctor Proctor said. He stopped and scanned the room, but neither he nor Lisa could spot the secret informant. Nilly wasn't looking around at all; he was too preoccupied studying this strange wax figure. The man was wearing a short sequined jacket. One of the figure's hands was positioned over its crotch, exactly like soccer players forming a wall for a free kick. He was holding his hat with his other hand, which was wearing a silver glove.

"Is that an aiming glove?" Nilly asked, squinting. "Why is he standing in that weird position?"

"Silly," Lisa said. "That glove was his signature. He's moonwalking."

"Oh, right," Nilly said, and turned to the crowd, which was streaming past them. "But if this meeting is supposed to be so secret, why are we meeting somewhere that's as crowded as a Tokyo escalator?"

"Because you can hide in a crowd, the way fish hide in a school," the Michael Jackson figure said. "No one notices who you're talking to, and there's so much noise that no one can hear what you're saying."

"I wasn't talking to you, Michael," Nilly said.

"What?" Lisa said.

"I said, I wasn't talking to him," Nilly said, pointing behind him with his thumb.

Lisa turned around and realized that it wasn't so much that the figure looked like Michael Jackson as that it looked so *alive*. So alive that it actually seemed totally normal when it kept talking.

"Now listen up, because both my legs are going to cramp up any minute, okay?" said Michael Jackson. "You'll find the Crunch Brothers at a pub in Eastburnwickside

called the Lion, the Hamster, and the Very Crooked Oxcart of Mr. Woomblenut Who Used to Sell Rye Beer Down by the Old Mill."

"I'm sorry," Lisa said. "I forgot to concentrate. Can you repeat that?"

"Just take a taxi and say you're going to the Lion on Buck Street," Michael Jackson whispered. "Now, get out of here before I collapse."

Doctor Proctor said, "Come on," and started to walk away.

"Hey, Michael," Nilly said. "Could I . . . uh, get your autograph?"

"Come on!" Lisa said, pulling Nilly along with her after Doctor Proctor. "He's dead!"

"Dead? He was just talking to us!"

"No, Michael Jackson! That guy isn't the real . . . oh, just come on!" Lisa said.

"But I want a souvenir! Please?" Nilly pleaded.

"Come on, Nilly!" she hissed.

Pouting a little, Nilly followed the other two. But by the exit he stopped, lit up again, and pointed.

"Like that! I want one of those!" Nilly exclaimed.

At a counter, there were wax museum souvenirs and celebrity masks for sale.

"Well, hurry up, then," Doctor Proctor said.

Nilly pushed his way over to the counter. "Excuse me, my lovely lady," he said to the saleslady, who was standing with her back to him, filing her nails. She turned and looked around at the air over Nilly's head, surprised not to see anyone.

"Down here, O Eiffel Tower of a woman," Nilly said, waving from down below.

She noticed him and lit up with a smile.

"One Napoléon mask, please!" he said.

"Sorry, my little friend, but we're sold out of Napoléon."

"Hmm." Nilly rubbed his chin. "Do you have any other small people who tried to achieve world domination? What about Julius Caesar? Genghis Khan? Adolf Hitler? Alexander the Great? Or should we say Alexander the Small?"

JULIUS CAESAR

MAXIMUS RUBLOV

GENGHIS KHAN

ADOLF HITLER

"Well," she said. "Unfortunately, things have kind of been picked over here, but we do have Maximus Rublov."

"Did he achieve world domination?" Nilly asked.

"Well, he did just buy the Houses of Parliament and half the rest of England. Plus, he owns the Chelchester City soccer team, so we made a mask of him for the World Cup finals."

She pointed to a shelf of blue Chelchester City soccer jerseys and replicas of the trophy in case you wanted to take one home and claim you were the cup winner. Next to that there was a mask of a guy with a prominent forehead, a receding hairline, narrow eyebrows that appeared to have been shaved with painstaking precision, and a goatee.

"*That's* Rublov? Do you have anyone a little more attractive who achieved world domination?" Nilly asked. "A little more like me?"

"Oh, as long as a man has charisma, people don't care that much about what he looks like, you know," the saleslady laughed. "And it's a well-known fact that nothing gives you more charisma than money."

"Then I'll take it!" Nilly said.

The Lion, the Hamster, and ... Look, It's a Long Name, So Just Read the Chapter, Okay?

AS USUAL, IT was super noisy in the pub we're just planning to call "the Lion." The bartender was standing by the tap handles taking beer orders while people toasted, talked about rugby, Hillman engines, and how many goals Chelchester City would beat Rotten Ham by in the final World Cup game. Stuff like that. Things they *weren't* talking about included hand-stitched handbags, French perfume, and the most recent royal wedding. As you may have guessed, there were more men than women in the Lion. A few of them were singing a song about how it was an irritatingly long way to go to a place called Tipperary, but suddenly all the singing and chatting in the place stopped. Because someone yanked the door open, its hinges moaning loudly, and slammed it shut again.

A tiny little guy wearing a tweed coat and a— well, as we already determined—very stupid-looking deerstalker hat stood there in the doorway. He took a tobacco pipe out of his mouth, marched over to the bar, climbed up onto one of the towering bar stools, and gave the bartender a stern look.

"My good man, give me the strongest soda you have."

The bartender kept polishing the glass, which already looked very clean. "The strongest, sir?"

"Don't you understand English?" Nilly said, taking off his hat and setting it on the bar. "I don't want the normal watery swill, I need something that will pick me up. Something that will bubble in my nose and scratch up my throat so it feels like I poured an anthill down there. On the rocks, no seltzer."

"Um, you could have a cola with ice and a slice of lemon?" the bartender suggested.

"Great. But make it a double," Nilly replied.

"A double, sir?"

"TWO slices of lemon, you party pooper!" Nilly said, spinning around on his stool and taking a closer look at the pub and its clientele, who were still staring at him. Then, loudly enough for everyone to hear, he said, "And don't even try giving me Diet Coke, or I'll shoot your party-pooper head right off your body, understand?"

The bartender filled a glass and set it in front of Nilly, who grabbed it, tilted his head back, opened wide, drained it in one go, and slammed the empty glass back down on the bar.

"Hit me again," Nilly groaned, pointing at the glass, his eyes bulging and his voice sounding oddly choked up from the carbonation.

The bartender filled it again, and Nilly tossed it right back.

A man in a hat that said MILLWALL on it had walked up to the bar and taken a seat next to Nilly.

"You play hard, stranger," the man said in a whiskey voice.

"Hard is the only way I play," Nilly said, looking at the reflection of the man's face in the mirror behind the shelves with the bottles on them.

"What are you doing here? You don't look like you're from around here," the man said.

"Rumor has it that this is where the best dart players

this side of the Thames can be found," Nilly said with a shrug.

"And so what if that is the case?"

"I'm the best dart player from the *other* side of the Thames," Nilly said, snatching a toothpick and starting to chew on it. "I'm looking to challenge him."

The man in front of him laughed briefly. "You? You're so small. How good a shot can you be?"

Nilly spit the toothpick into his empty cola glass. "Care to find out?"

"No thanks, little guy," the man said, and pulled off his cap. "Charlie Crunch don't steal chump change from pipsqueaks."

Nilly stared at the man's shaved head, the unibrow, the letter *C* tattooed on his forehead. "Let me guess. You're Charlie Crunch."

"Maybe."

"And what if I say I have fifty pounds with a picture of the queen on it in my pocket?" Nilly asked.

The boy and the man eyed each other. And without looking so much as a millimeter away, Nilly plucked a peanut out of the dish on the counter, tossed it up in the air, tilted his head back quick as lightning, and flipped his mouth open so wide that his jaws creaked. The peanut reached its peak and started coming down again. Nilly crossed his bulging eyes, following the peanut's progress. Everyone else in the place crossed their eyes too. They were all staring at that peanut as it fell and fell and fell. All the way down until it hit the tip of Nilly's little upturned nose and bounced off.

"Ha!" Nilly cried, straightening back up again. "Did you see that? Bull's-eye every time!" He pointed triumphantly to the tip of his nose.

An astonished murmur spread through the pub.

"Let's see your money, little guy," Charlie Crunch said, laughing out loud.

Nilly pulled a big, smooth bill out of his pants pocket and slapped it on the counter.

"I guess I do take money from little pipsqueaks after all," Charlie Crunch said, and then laughed loudly. "Let's play darts."

NILLY AND CHARLIE Crunch took their positions a little over seven feet from the face of the dartboard (to be totally accurate: seven feet, nine and one-quarter inches, which, according to the World Darts Federation, is the recognized standard distance, after all). The other pub patrons clustered around them and watched attentively as Charlie squinted one eye shut, aimed with the dart pinched between his index finger and his thumb—and threw.

THUNK!

The onlookers cheered. The dart had pierced the field that said twenty. It was the highest number on the board. But Charlie's dart was sort of on the outside.

Nilly stepped up to the line.

"You're going to throw with a *mitten* on your hand?" Charlie scoffed.

Nilly didn't respond. He just aimed for the red dot right in the middle of the board. Bent his arm back. And threw.

THUNK!

The dart stood there quivering, as close to the middle of the board as you could possibly get.

"Ha-ha!" Nilly cried. "Eat dust, Charlie Crunch, now you're the NEXT BEST dart player this side of the Thames!"

"Don't you even know the rules, little guy?" Charlie asked, raising an eyebrow. "That only gives you fifty points. My dart hit the triple twenty part, which makes sixty."

"Huh?" Nilly responded. "Oh yeah. Of course I knew that. I . . . uh, just wanted to give you a little head start to make things exciting."

"Thanks," Charlie said, taking his position and

throwing. *THUNK!* Another triple twenty.

Nilly leaned over and whispered to one of the people watching, a man in a sixpence cap with no front teeth, "Little bit of a brain fart here, um. What's the most points you can get in one throw again?"

"Triple twenty," the toothless man said.

"Of course," Nilly said, and aimed. And threw. *THUNK!* His dart landed right next to Charlie Crunch's two.

"Triple twenty!" the audience cheered. Charlie had 120, Nilly had 110.

But before the cheers had died down, Charlie stepped up and threw, and his dart landed so close to his first two that all three darts quivered together for a bit.

"Triple twenty!" the audience cried. Charlie raised both hands over his head and accepted the audience's cheers.

Nilly stepped up and aimed.

"You don't need to throw," the toothless guy said. "There's no way you can get as many points as—"

But Nilly had already thrown. His dart landed on the triple twenty, and so close to the other darts this time that one of them fell out and dropped to the floor.

A murmur ran through the crowd.

"All right, all right," Nilly said, pulling the bill out of his pocket and passing it to Charlie, who was staring at him, his face bright red.

"Are you trying to piss me off, little guy?" Charlie snarled.

"Huh?" Nilly looked innocently up at Charlie, who looked like he was thinking about strangling Nilly.

"You won!" the toothless man whispered into Nilly's ear. "The dart that fell down was his. That means he loses those points. Do you *really* not know the rules?"

"No, but seriously, Charlie," Nilly said. "I was just wondering if you could break a two-hundred pound note for me. So I could buy you a drink."

Charlie Crunch cocked his head to the side and said, "Something's not right here. This guy doesn't know the rules, and yet he plays darts like a world champion. No, better than a world champion. Wearing a mitten!" Charlie grabbed Nilly by the hair, picked him straight up, and held him out in front of himself at arm's length. "Who are you really? How did you know I'd be here? Are you—"

He was interrupted by a remarkably Scottish-sounding cry from one of the tables in the very back.

"Jings, crivvens! Is no' that Tartan-Sherl, the world-famous bank robber?"

Everyone in the room turned to see who'd said that.

There was a tall, skinny man with a beard sitting at that table, wearing something that looked suspiciously like a wig, and something that looked even more suspiciously like a pair of swim goggles. Sitting next to him was a girl with a nose so huge you almost had to believe she'd glued it on. Beneath her nose there was a small, yet thick and bushy, mustache. Not the kind of thing you see on a little girl every day.

"Quiet, you two!" Nilly urged them. "Don't give me away!"

"Um, that's exactly what we're doing!" the girl yelled. "We're GIVING you away!"

"Uh," Nilly said. "Uh . . ." He leaned over to the toothless man. "Uh, I'm having a little brain fart here. What was my next line?"

"Huh?" the toothless man said.

"I see, laddie, that you . . . uh, dunna know what you're supposed to say now," the skinny man at the table said, standing up. "Well, I'm gonnae call Scotland

Yard and have them coom and arrest you. Yes, by golly if I'm not going to do that right now, unless someone stops me with a blow or a kick. A really hard kick. But who would do that?"

"Oh, that was it!" Nilly whispered. Then he pushed his way through the crowded room, jumped up onto that table, raised one of his feet, and slammed his heel down onto the tabletop.

A new murmur ran through the pub with the way-too-long name as the table split in two with a deafening *crack*. Followed by yet another murmur as a second blow from the dart champion's heel split the table into four pieces. Then eight. Then sixteen. Then . . . well, what do you think?

Then Nilly started kicking the table fragments, which sailed through the air to eventually end up as a neatly stacked little woodpile next to the bar. Then he turned to the Scottish man and the girl with the weird nose and the mustache, who was shaking, backed up against the wall, holding her index finger up in the air in warning.

"You're not going to call the police now after all, are you?" Nilly warned. "You won't if you know what's good for you."

"Yes, Tartan-Sherl," the girl squeaked in a voice so pathetic you would almost think she was just pretending to be afraid. "You're such a dastardly villain, and we're so scared we're about to wet our pants. And since we know what's good for us, well . . . well . . ." The girl exhaled into her mustache a couple of times and looked like she was trying to remember the rest of her lines, before she finally continued, "We'll just leave now without calling anyone."

"Excellent!" Nilly said. "And since I'm in a good mood today, I'm going to let you go without kicking your sorry party-pooper heads off. Get out of here!"

And precisely—or at least more or less precisely— two seconds later, they were out the door.

Nilly turned to the astonished crowd and flung up his arms in victory. "Bartender, a round of your strongest soda for everyone! My treat! Put the table on my tab too! And pour a little of something extra good for my new friend Charlie here!"

"But—" Charlie began.

"No, I absolutely *refuse* to take any money from you, Charlie. I have way too much money as it is!" Nilly said.

Charlie Crunch eyed Nilly uncertainly for a second. Then he lit up in a big smile.

"Let me at least buy you a beer. How about a Guinness, Tartan-Sherl?" Charlie asked.

"Thanks, Charlie, but I only drink . . . uh, the hard stuff," Nilly said.

The two sat down at a table and were served a cola and a beer.

"So, you're in the bank-robbing business too, eh?" Charlie said, wiping beer foam off his upper lip.

"Yup," Nilly said. "I'm always on the lookout for

other robbers who'd like to team up on crime sprees with a skilled bandit like myself."

"What a shame," Charlie said with a shrug. "We only collaborate with people with a proven track record of real robberies."

"Oh yeah?" Nilly said, setting down his glass. "And just how do they do that?"

"They invite us along on a crime spree that *they* planned, not the other way around."

"Oh, I see," Nilly said, and then burped loudly. "Of course, I've got a few upcoming crime sprees planned."

"You do?"

"Sure, I'm a robber, aren't I?" Nilly said.

"Like what?"

"Like . . . uh, the easiest money you can imagine. It'll be like snatching it from old ladies and babies."

"*Like what*, I said!" Charlie said impatiently.

"Snatching it from old ladies and babies, I said!" Nilly repeated.

"Could you be a little more specific, little guy?"

"Well, yeah. There's this, uh, old lady, you see. And this kid, you know?" Nilly began.

Charlie leaned so far over the table that the C on his forehead almost touched the tips of Nilly's red hair. "Yes?"

"Yeah, well uh, she's . . . uh, the kid's grandmother, and she usually takes her for a walk in her stroller through Hyde Park every morning around nine o'clock."

"Where's the money in that?" Charlie asked skeptically.

"In the stroller."

"The stroller?"

"Yeah. This grandmother is filthy rich, but terrified of being burglarized. So she takes the money with her whenever she takes the kid for a walk," Nilly said, and then leaned back in his chair and took a swig of his cola. "The grandmother thinks, 'Who would have the heart to rob an old lady and baby in broad daylight?' And who would have the heart to do that?"

"Heh, heh, heh," Charlie snickered. "I know someone. Okay, give me the details, little guy."

"I HAD TO come up with the details on the spot," Nilly explained later, lying on the sofa back in their hotel room as Doctor Proctor removed his wig and Lisa pulled off her fake nose with its attached mustache. "So I said this grandmother would be in Hyde Park at nine o'clock tomorrow morning."

"And you expect *us* to play the part of the grandmother and grandchild?" Lisa said with a groan, and then went into the bathroom to brush her teeth, because it was bedtime for hardworking secret agents.

"With a stroller full of money?" Doctor Proctor said with a sigh, pulling on his nightcap.

"Hey, I had to come up with something!" Nilly said, taking off his socks. "If this goes well, Charlie promised I could go on one of their robberies. And once I'm a part of their gang, I can start pumping them for information, right?" Nilly sniffed his socks and made a face.

"Where are we going to get the money to fill a baby carriage by tomorrow morning?" Lisa asked. "If we're supposed to be in the park by nine, the banks won't even be open yet!"

Nilly clasped his hands behind his head and contemplated his toes. "Relax, I have a solution. Just trust *Tartan-Sherl*, people!"

Doctor Proctor blushed and said, "Aam sorry about that, Nilly. I was trying to call you T-O-R-D-E-N-S-K-J-O-L-D, after the most famous Norwegian naval hero of all time. But, hech, ever since I took that multi-lingual pill, my tongue just cannae handle some of the Norwegian sounds anymair."

Lisa popped her head out of the bathroom door and stopped brushing her teeth for a minute. "Did you just say you have a solution, Nilly? Great," she said sarcastically. "The only thing we can count on is that it's probably a plan where *you* have all the fun and get to be the hero!" She disappeared back into the bathroom, and they heard more brushing noises.

"Lisa," Nilly said. "Of course it will be fun for you, too. You get to play the lead part tomorrow."

"I do?" Lisa called, and for a bit it was quiet from the bathroom. Until she called, "What if something goes wrong tomorrow?"

"Relax, this is a watertight, bulletproof plan," Nilly said. "Nothing's going to go wrong! Because there's nothing that *can* go wrong!"

And after that Nilly didn't think there was much more to discuss. And neither did Big Ben, apparently, because it struck eleven times. And fifteen minutes later they were all in their beds. They may not all have fallen asleep right away. But by the time Big Ben struck twelve, *then* they were all asleep.

The Itty-Bitty
Little Robbery

THE MORNING SUN shone on the large park in the middle of London named Hyde Park, and it was exactly—no, not exactly—it was *about* nine o'clock. An old woman was walking with a baby carriage along one of the paths that crisscrosses the park.

You could see someone sitting on a bench holding a

newspaper in front of him- or herself. The strange thing was that when you looked more closely, the hand that was holding the left side of the paper was large and hairy, while the hand holding the right was tiny, hairless, and very pale. The newspaper was the *Daily Observer of Times*, the thickest, widest newspaper in the Western Hemisphere. And if we had had X-ray vision and could see through all the pages about British politicians who'd done something wrong, floral decorations in Harrogate, and the Rotten Ham team's soccer coach, who was actually a krill fisherman who had never played soccer before, we would see that there weren't just one or two, but *four*, people hidden behind the paper.

They happened to be sitting in alphabetical order. Alfie, Betty, Charlie. And Maximus Rublov. Wait! Rublov was here? Well, at any rate, it was a tiny little guy who was the very spitting image of Rublov.

"Is that them, Sherl?" Alfie whispered.

No response.

"Sherl!"

"Oh, right, that's me," the tiny little guy said, adjusting his Rublov mask.

"I asked if that odd woman over there with the baby carriage is her!" Alfie said.

Rublov—who actually was Sherl (who actually was Nilly)—peeked out from behind the newspaper. "Yes, that's them. Synchronize your watches!"

"Why?"

"Because it's . . . uh, good to have synchronized watches. . . ."

"Get on with it, shrimp!" Alfie ordered.

"Yes. Yes, of course."

Nilly let go of the paper, hopped down off the park bench, and ran toward the baby carriage, yelling so that everyone around them could hear his words loud and clear: "This is a masked robbery in broad daylight! Give me the baby carriage right now, or it doesn't look good for you! Or your grandchild!"

The odd woman adjusted her dress, bonnet, and swim goggles, and then called back just as loudly and clearly, "Terrible! Awful! Don't shoot me with that . . . uh, pistol." And then added in a much quieter voice, "Where is the pistol you were supposed to have?"

"They didn't have a gun I could borrow," Nilly whispered back. "Just pretend to faint!"

And with that the odd old woman collapsed in the grass, her skirt sliding up to reveal a pair of unusually thin and hairy legs.

Nilly leaned over the baby carriage and looked down at Lisa's face. She was wearing a baby bonnet and sucking on a big pink pacifier. She looked furious.

"You call this the lead role?" she hissed.

Nilly grabbed hold of her and tried to lift her out.

"Put up a little resistance, would you!" he whispered.

Lisa hit him on the head hard and started bawling.

"Not *that* much resistance!" Nilly moaned. "And help

me get you out of the carriage, you weigh half a ton!"

With that they both tumbled over backward, and Lisa rolled away across the grass, screeching at the top of her lungs.

"Hey there!" they heard a man's voice call out. "What's going on?"

Nilly got up onto his feet, grabbed the baby carriage, and started walking.

"Stop!"

Nilly turned around. There was a man in a black uniform. At first Nilly thought he must be a knight who had misplaced his horse, since he had a black helmet on his head and a riding crop in his hand. But then he realized this was serious and started to run.

"Stop in the name of the law!" the man yelled.

It was a policeman!

Nilly's heart started beating just as fast as his short legs were drumming against the ground behind the baby carriage.

"Coppers!" he hissed as he ran past the park bench. The *Daily Observer of Times* was flung up into the air, and three men in jeans and suspenders came running up alongside Nilly and the baby carriage.

They heard a whistle blow behind them.

"He's got reinforcements," Charlie panted.

Nilly turned to look, and sure enough, now there were three policemen running behind them. And the police were gaining on them. And yet the Crunch Brothers started slowing down.

"Faster!" Nilly said. "What are you guys doing?"

"We're bank robbers," Charlie wheezed. "We're out of shape."

They were approaching a downhill slope, and the policemen were only six or seven yards behind them.

"Hop in!" Nilly said, jumping into the baby carriage.

"Huh?" Charlie said.

"Hop in, now!"

And with that, the three brothers jumped into the

baby carriage, and they started careening down the hill. Alfie and Betty were each clinging tightly to a side, while Charlie was sitting in the baby carriage with his legs dangling off the back. Nilly was sitting in front, trying to steer by leaning left or right. They were moving faster and faster, and the wobbly little baby carriage tipped ominously each time Nilly had to turn to keep them on the narrow asphalt path. Eventually the path widened a little, and Nilly looked back at the policemen, who were getting smaller and smaller, and finally gave up running.

"Yippee!" Nilly cried, closing his eyes and enjoying the feel of the wind and the sun through the holes in his rubber mask.

"Uh, Sherl . . . ," Alfie said.

Delightful wind, delightful speed, delightful freedom.

"Sherl!" Alfie said with more urgency.

"Oh, right, that's me, isn't it?" Nilly said, opening

his eyes. The baby carriage had slowed. They were at the bottom of the hill, and there were five policemen blocking the path ahead of them with their arms crossed.

"Hang on!" Nilly said, hopping over to the left side and up onto the top of Alfie's bowler hat, jamming it down over Alfie's eyes.

"I can't see!" Alfie wailed, flailing his arms as the baby carriage suddenly veered left. So suddenly that Nilly and the bowler hat were about to fly off, when Betty grabbed the lapel of Nilly's tweed jacket at the very last instant and held on to him.

They raced out of the park, onto a paved pedestrian square. The crowd leaped aside, and they almost knocked down a man who was standing on top of a crate, screaming that the end of the world was coming. Nilly couldn't have agreed more, because just then they rolled into a street, quite a busy street, with cars and buses speeding toward them, every last one of them on the *wrong* side of the road! This was England, after all.

They were one second away from being mashed by an enormous white Rolls-Royce!

Nilly took a deep breath and leaped over to Betty's head, frantically clawing at his smooth, bald head, and just as he was losing his hold, he managed to grab Betty's nostril with both hands. He heard the middle brother groan as the baby carriage turned to avoid the oncoming traffic at the very last moment, careening over to the opposite side of the street. Where they rolled right over to the back of a red double-decker bus and came to a stop with a gentle *bump*.

"Phew!" said Nilly.

"Phew!" said Betty.

"Where are we? What's happening?" Alfie cried, tugging at his bowler hat, trying to pull it back up so he could see.

"We have to get out of here!" Charlie said.

They turned around and saw the five policemen running across the street toward them. Three of them

had lost their comical helmets, but none of them had lost their batons. They were blowing their whistles, their angry faces bright red, and they generally did not look anything like the policemen Nilly had seen in the London tourist brochures. There was exactly zero chance that he and the out-of-shape Crunch Brothers were going to get away.

The bus started, and Nilly coughed from the exhaust. Then, to his surprise, he felt them starting to move again.

He turned and saw Betty Crunch grinning at him. Betty had grabbed hold of the pole that served as a handrail by the back door of the bus, which had now suddenly become their tow truck.

A voice came over the loudspeaker in the bus ceiling. "Welcome to this guided tour of London. If you'll look to your right, you'll see Speaker's Corner and Hyde Park. We'll be driving past Trafalgar Square, Buckingham Palace, and . . ."

The policemen behind them had stopped running and were standing, doubled over forward with their hands on their knees, huffing and puffing so their backs went up and down.

"Yippee!" Nilly yelled for the second time that day, even though it only ten past nine in the morning.

A face appeared over the roof of the bus. "Forget about Speaker's Corner! Look who's down there, everyone! It's Maximus Rublov!"

More faces appeared over the edge of the roof. Apparently there were seats on the roof deck up there.

"Hi, Rublov!" another tourist called. "What's the matter? Can't you afford a bus ticket?"

"Not if I'm going to buy Ibranaldovez!" Nilly yelled, standing up in the baby carriage and bowing gallantly.

Nilly suddenly lost his balance as the baby carriage swung to the left and disconnected from the bus.

Now Nilly and the Crunch Brothers were racing

down a cobblestone alley that got narrower and narrower and darker and darker the farther down it they went. The cobblestones made Nilly's teeth chatter in his mouth.

"W-h-e-r-e a-r-e w-e?" he managed to say.

Just then the baby carriage whipped to the right, right into the brick wall of a building, and just at the very instant Nilly was sure they would crash, a trapdoor opened and they rolled down a walkway, coming out on the floor of a cellar, bumping right into a big, black pile of coal.

"We're home!" Charlie announced.

Nilly coughed, climbed out of the now overturned baby carriage, and rubbed the soot out of his eyes. And as he stood there rubbing, he noticed how quiet it had gotten. No one said a word. There must be something in the room that was keeping the otherwise very chatty brothers from . . .

Nilly opened his eyes. He was looking right at a

pair of legs that were at least as hairy as the ones he'd just seen in the park, but thick like tree trunks. Nilly slowly looked up, higher and higher, as the hairs on the back of his neck stood up.

"Mama," Charlie whispered.

She whose name could only be whispered had some humongous arms on her, which were crossed over her humongous chest, and above that there was a woman's head, which looked like it had come out of a waffle iron, because it was as wide as a snowplow and covered in layer upon layer of superfluous, wrinkled skin. And a pair of staring, glowing hunk-of-coal-like eyes in between the wrinkles.

"Mama," whispered Betty.

There was a little *pop* sound as Alfie finally managed to pull the bowler hat back off his head and see again.

"Mama," he whispered.

But the woman wasn't paying any attention to them. Her eyes were focused on the little redhead.

"So," she said, her voice sounding like an average dragon with a slightly above average anger management problem and an ugly, advanced case of laryngitis. "What are you?" she croaked.

"I'm—I'm—" Nilly began, his voice trembling, "I'm Nil—Sherl! I'm Sherl! And I'm a bandit. But not one of those trustworthy bandits. A regular bandit down to the core, actually."

"Good for you," the woman said, leaning down toward Nilly. And what do you know if she didn't have dragon breath, too. "Because I'm . . . ," she began, and then lowered her voice to a crackling whisper right next to Nilly's ear, "Mama Crunch."

"Gulp!" Nilly said, quite involuntarily.

"And I hope you're not a sissy, Mr. Sherl, because it's time to eat now. Got it?"

Sherl looked around at the other three, who looked really terrified.

"Uh . . . I wonder what we're going to be eating, Mrs. Crunch?" Nilly said.

Mama Crunch straightened up and laughed a laugh that sounded like someone trying to start a car when it's minus twenty degrees outside.

"Yes, I bet you do."

The Truth About
Monopolynesia

NILLY AND THE Crunch Brothers were sitting around the dining table. It turned out the room had tilted a little to the northwest ever since a bomb had gone right through the roof during World War II. The bomb hadn't exploded, but it crushed the coffee table and had broken both lenses of Grandpa Crunch's eyeglasses and his almost-full whiskey glass. He'd nodded off on the sofa after a little afternoon looting. Not much had changed in the living room since then. Even the windows were still covered with the blackout curtains that had been hung up to keep German soldiers from spotting any lights from the buildings to help them aim. Now the blackout curtains were to keep anyone from Scotland Yard or anyone else from looking in and figuring out where the Crunch Brothers lived. The only light in the leaning living room came from the coal-burning stove.

"Act like you like it," Charlie whispered, stuffing a mouthful of food into his mouth and jabbing Nilly, who was sitting still, staring at the plate Mama Crunch had slapped down in front of him and told him was bottom fish and toenail chips.

"Uh, what's the sauce?" Nilly asked, poking his fork into something gray and slimy that was covering the fish.

"That's called Grandfather's Cough," Charlie said, and then made a face as he took a bite. "But I don't think grandfather's actual sputum tastes so—"

"Shh!" Alfie said.

They were listening to the sounds from the kitchen, where Mama Crunch was still boiling and sizzling away.

"It was worse yesterday," Charlie said. "We had hot dogs."

"Hot dogs?" Nilly asked. "Like in a bun?"

"More like a heated-up bulldog with cauliflower and rickets. This tastes like—"

They were interrupted by Betty leaning over and vomiting under the edge of the table.

Alfie nodded toward Nilly's plate. "There's no way out, Sherl. It's better for you to eat Grandfather's Cough than to have to deal with"—he dropped his voice to a whisper—"Mama." He raised his voice again. "Believe me."

"I see," Nilly said, staring at his plate. "Well, then I guess I'd better get it over with. . . ."

"That's it exactly," Charlie said.

"That's what exactly?" Nilly asked.

"Unfortunately, it's not over with when we eat this up."

"It's not? What happens after that?" Nilly asked.

"The worst part," Alfie said in a deep, funereal voice that made the water glasses rattle.

"The Birmingham pudding," the brothers all said in unison.

"Shh," Betty said. "She's coming. . . ."

The kitchen door opened, and Mama Crunch's enormous body came in. She was marching straight toward Nilly.

"What is this?" she wheezed, dragon stench pouring out of her enormous mouth.

Nilly quickly stuffed his fork into his mouth.

"I had to admire the way the food looked first, Mrs. Crunch," Nilly said, chewing slowly. "Delightful bottom fish, Mrs. Crunch, melts on the tongue! And you simply *must* tell me how you got the toenail chips so crunchy and the Grandfather's Cough so . . . uh, slimy."

"I mean, what is *this*?!" the woman whose name shall only be whispered screamed, slapping a wad of bills onto the table. "The baby carriage was full of Monopoly money!"

All chewing and plate clinking suddenly stopped. And everyone stared at Nilly.

"Monopoly money?" Alfie hissed, squeezing one eye shut and slowly licking the long, black-handled knife he was holding in his hand.

"Ahem, yes, isn't it great?" Nilly said, reveling in his packing brilliance. "Real Monopoly money."

"But that's not worth anything!" Betty said.

"It's not?" Nilly said, looking at Betty in surprise. Then he lit up. "Oh, you're thinking of the money they use in that game . . . what's it called again?"

He looked around but did not receive an answer, just threatening looks from dark-red faces all around.

"Monopoly!" Nilly exclaimed. "Oh, but that's fake Monopoly money. This is real Monopoly money."

"What's the difference?" Charlie asked.

"Well, obviously these authentic bills have watermarks in them," Nilly said.

Alfie set his bowler hat back on his head and then

held one of the bills up to the light. "I don't see any watermark," he said.

"Of course not," Nilly said. "It's made of water."

"What kind of nonsense is this?" Mama Crunch said. "Monopoly money is play money whether it's fake or real."

"That's actually a very common misunderstanding, Mrs. Crunch," Nilly said, holding up a toenail chip. It was yellow and white and looked exactly like a . . . well, an old, well-used toenail. "But when they created the game of Monopoly, they copied the money used in Monopolynesia."

"Monopolynesia?" Mama Crunch repeated, lowering her arms to her sides in a way that allowed Nilly to see her bulging biceps.

"Yup," Nilly said, crunching a toenail chip between his teeth and smiling quickly.

"There is no country called Monopolynesia," Alfie said quietly.

Nilly chewed and chewed. Then he said, "If the Monopolyppians could hear you now, they would be really insulted, Alfie."

"Oh yeah?" Alfie said. Then he lifted his chin and pulled his knife across his throat, making a scraping sound. Short, black crumbs of stubble sprinkled onto his fish like pepper. "And what would they do about that?"

"Probably not that much," Nilly said with a shrug. "Because they're shy, you know, the Monopolyppians. And so small. Their country is just a small atoll in the Pacific somewhere between Togaparty and Danish Guano."

Just then Nilly felt something big, heavy, and warm settle around the back of his neck. Mama Crunch had taken a seat in the chair next to him, and the arm she wrapped around him made Nilly think of an enormous anaconda snake he had once encountered.

"Listen up, Mr. Sherl. My boys might not be the

brightest geography students. But unfortunately for you, I went to middle school *and* housewifery school. And I've *never* heard of Monopolynesia! So I'm going to chop you up into little pieces and put you in the birdcage. Alfie, give me the knife. . . ."

"With all due respect, Mrs. Crunch," Nilly said, laughing hysterically as his heart pounded like a piece of cardboard in some bicycle spokes. "Remember that Monopolynesia is so small that the country doesn't even have a seat at the UN. They just have a standing spot all the way in the back. Without any voting rights and no key to the restrooms. And if any army attacks Monopolynesia, no other country would help them, because what good could possibly come from being on the same side as such a small, insignificant country? That's how it's always been for those of us who are small in stature." Nilly looked up at Mama Crunch with his most sorrowful expression. "And that's why the Monopolyppians hide and pretend they don't exist.

There's hardly any information about the country anywhere."

Mama Crunch took the knife Alfie handed her and squeezed her arm around Nilly a little more tightly. "I see, Mr. Sherl. You're claiming that a whole country is managing to keep itself a secret?"

"You guys don't believe me?" Nilly asked, his voice sounding a little choked up. "Try Google, then! If you find anything on there about the country of Monopolynesia, I'll give you my share of the loot. And that's not small potatoes, because last time I checked the exchange rate, one Monopoly was worth thirteen point one nine English pounds."

Mama Crunch placed the tip of the knife against Nilly's throat. Nilly gulped and felt his Adam's apple scrape the tip of the knife on its way up *and* down. He shut his eyes and waited to be turned into bird food.

"Check it, Charlie," the dragon voice commanded.

Nilly heard fingers tapping on a cell phone while

Mama Crunch's arm squeezed even harder around his neck. He was going to lose consciousness soon. The room went completely silent. Nilly opened his eyes. Everything was black. Had he passed out already? Had he been strangled? Kaput, finished, finito? It smelled weird. This couldn't be heaven, unless heaven smelled like wet socks that had been sitting in a plastic bag for a long time.

"Sherl's right," he heard a voice say from far away. "Not one hit for the country of Monopolynesia."

The pressure let up. And Nilly realized his whole head was being pushed up into Mama Crunch's naked armpit. Then the arm was gone, it got light again, and Nilly started gasping for air.

"There, you see?" he wheezed. "Do you believe me now?"

"Hmm," Mama Crunch said, using the knife as a toothpick. "We'll find out soon enough if the money is worth anything. Come on, let's take it to the bank and see if we can exchange it for proper English pounds."

"No, no, are you crazy?!" Nilly yelled. "If we exchange it now, Scotland Yard will trace the money back to us. What we have to do is put the money into a bank account here in London and then order money laundering through Switzerland. Then we can change it back into English pounds when the money comes back, freshly laundered, in a few days."

"LAUNDER the money?" Charlie exclaimed. "Are you crazy? It'll shrink!"

"There, there, Charlie," Mama Crunch said. "Money laundering just means confusing the stupid police by sending the money on a little goose chase so they can't figure out where it originally came from."

"Exactly," Nilly said, even though he wasn't *totally* clear on how money laundering actually worked. "How did you guys think I was still on the loose, anyway? I launder myself from head to toe every other Friday. It's recommended for all robbers."

"Hmm," Mama said. "The stuff the little one is saying might not be so dumb after all. We'll go deposit the money at the bank. But if there's anything fishy at all, then we're not feeding you to the birds, Mr. Sherl."

"You're not?" Nilly said with a gulp.

"No, you won't get out of it that easily. We'll take you straight to the poker table," Mama Crunch said.

"Blood knuckles." Charlie chuckled.

"Come on, let's go to the bank," Alfie said.

"Hey there, not so fast!" Mama Crunch said, holding up her hand. "First we have to eat the Birmingham pudding."

She went to the kitchen.

"Nice try, Alfie," Betty whispered, and then sighed heavily.

Then the kitchen door opened again and Mama Crunch came back in with a big serving dish of something quivering and trembling, like a moon jellyfish that someone had inflated with a bicycle pump.

"Dig in!"

Nilly looked at his plate, where the dragon had placed a large dollop. There was no way out. He picked up his spoon and scooped up a little bit. Closed his eyes. Stuck the spoon in his mouth and thought about Jell-O with all his might. He thought about it so hard that he could not only taste the Jell-O taste, but he could hear the birds singing in Doctor Proctor's pear tree and his friends chatting, the sun warming his face, and the joy of knowing there was still at least five feet of Jell-O left on the serving platter. He took another spoonful, larger this time. And another.

"Glglm," Nilly said with his mouth full. "What a delightful pudding, my lovely Mrs. Crunch! You simply *must* give me the recipe, otherwise I'm afraid I'll have to steal it from you."

Nilly looked up at Mama Crunch, who was standing over him with her arms crossed. He watched the vigilant expression on her face change first to disbelief.

And as he took yet another bite, how it sort of cracked, and you could—if you really looked closely—see a tiny little smile in between all the folds of skin in that dour, pinched face.

It lasted one second. Then it was over.

"Enough eating!" she said. "We're going to the bank now!"

A Crazy Deposit

THE TIME WAS . . . I'm not actually quite sure what time it was, but it was kind of late in the day. And we're still in London. An old, rusty Hillman Spitfire Roadster was parked on Newscorphamtonshire Street, across from Midclay Barkland Gordon Banks. All right, that's plenty. There won't be any more of those long English names in this chapter.

Charlie Crunch was sitting behind the wheel and Nilly, aka Sherl, was next to him.

"Thanks for letting me borrow your gun," Nilly said.

"It's just a water pistol," Charlie said. "What do you need it for, though? You're just going to deposit the money."

"Old habits, you know," Nilly said, peering down into the bag with the Monopoly money. "We robbers feel naked in a bank without a gun."

Nilly took a deep breath and tried not to think about hungry birds or blood knuckles. Then he pulled on his Maximus Rublov mask, opened the car door, and jumped out. He looked around and ran across the rain-wet street. He checked his reflection in the glass door before entering the small, almost empty bank.

"How can I help you, sir?" the lady behind the counter asked when Nilly walked up and stood on his tiptoes in front of her to be seen.

"Oh, nothing much," Nilly said, pulling the water pistol out of his belt and putting it on the counter as he pushed a note through the glass window. It had taken him a long time to decide what it should say, and it occurred to him now that maybe he could have spent a bit more time on it. What it said was:

THIS IS A DEPOSIT! Accept this money, open an account, and give me a real receipt for 150,000 Monopolies. Yes, I know this currency doesn't actually exist, but just do as I say, otherwise I will shoot this gun, which you must not think is a toy. Read the rest of this note only if you're farsighted. Thank you.

Since you are still reading, that means you ARE farsighted and MAYBE you saw that it says "Made in Taiwan" on the gun. But you must know that they make real guns in Taiwan too, and this is NOT a toy gun. Cross my heart. Or cross my legs, anyway. Have a nice day.

She took a long time reading the note. Then she read it again. Then she shook her head and started typing on her keyboard.

Nilly looked around nervously and tried to smile casually at the surveillance camera on the ceiling and the guard who was standing over in the corner, half-asleep.

"Here you go, sir," the woman said, handing him a receipt. "And thank you for your business."

"THE MONEY IS in the account and everything is fine," Nilly said, digging into the fresh batch of Birmingham pudding Mama Crunch had placed before him.

"Wonderful," Betty said, reading the receipt. "We're rich!"

Betty laughed and elbowed Alfie and Charlie, who were sitting on either side of him at the dining table inside the Crunch family's living room with the blackout curtains drawn. Outside it had started and stopped raining three times and also gotten dark.

"Well, there's rich and then there's rich," Mama

Crunch said, grabbing the receipt. "We're not exactly millionaires. The rent and the heating bills don't exactly pay themselves, Mr. Sherl. London is superexpensive, almost as expensive as Tokyo. In a few days I'm going to be forced to send my boys back out to do some basic pickpocketing. Otherwise it's right back to Mr. Dickens's poorhouse for us."

"Well, we're monopolaires, anyway," Nilly said, shoveling in the Birmingham pudding. "And this is even better than Doctor Pro—uh, I mean Doctor MacKaroni's Jell-O, Mrs. Crunch. You wouldn't by any chance happen to have a little more, would you?"

Mama Crunch laughed, slapping Nilly hard enough on his back that his pudding almost came back up again, and then disappeared into the kitchen.

"Here!" Alfie said, holding out an enormous lit cigar for Nilly. "This is yours!"

Nilly accepted it and took a puff while making the V-is-for-victory sign with his fingers.

His face slowly turned blue.

"Well?" Alfie said.

And then bluer.

"Well?" Betty said.

Then a dark navy blue. A drop of sweat rolled down to the turned-up tip of his nose.

"Talk to us, Sherl," Charlie said, worried.

And when Nilly finally spoke, he did it while inhaling, so it sounded like a death rattle: "I like to live dangerously, so I'm going to smoke the rest of this at home in bed."

Nilly put the cigar out on his pudding plate and leaned his forehead lightly against the top of the table.

"Now that we're discussing danger," he said as the blue hue in his skin gradually faded. "Did you guys read about that diamond that was stolen in South Africa?" He raised his head and looked at the brothers. "Now *those* are robbers who like to live dangerously! I really wonder who could have done that, because that was impressive. Yes, yes . . ." Nilly helped himself to more pudding. "I suppose the world will never know who those super robbers are. . . ."

"Heh, heh," Charlie laughed, looking at his brothers. "Super robbers, did you guys hear that?"

"Heh, heh," Betty said. "We're not exactly small potatoes, huh?"

Nilly's spoon stopped halfway to his mouth. "What?" he said. "You're kidding. You don't mean that—that you guys—"

"Heh, heh," Alfie said. "And it wasn't just the diamond we stole either, eh, boys?"

"Not *just* the diamond?" Nilly exclaimed, astounded.

"Nope," said Alfie, putting out his own cigar. "Brazil's gold reserve. Norway's gold reserve. We struck in three different parts of the world in three weeks."

"You above-average hoodlums!" Nilly exclaimed. "You guys are my idols! Who'd you guys do all these jobs for?"

"Why are you asking about that?" Alfie said.

Nilly stuffed his spoon into his mouth. "You guys aren't smart enough to do this on your own, so . . ." Nilly stopped eating. Looked up. Found all three of them staring at him. "I mean *dumb* enough to do this on your own, heh-heh."

"So . . . ," Alfie said slowly. "Thaaaaat's what you meant?"

"'Course," Nilly said, gulping. "It's a lot smarter to just do the job and get paid for it than to be the *idiot* who has to store the diamond and all that gold while secret agents from at least three countries are trying to track it down. Right?"

"Oh," Charlie said. "The guy we did it for isn't as dumb as you think."

"Who was it?" Nilly quickly asked.

"You don't need to be sticking your peanut nose into that," Alfie said. "But it just so happens that he's storing the gold somewhere where *no one* can find it."

"Pooh," Nilly said. "Then it must be locked behind three thick armored doors in a bank vault so well protected that not even I could get in there."

"Heh-heh," Charlie laughed.

"Heh-heh," Betty laughed.

"Heh-heh," Alfie laughed.

"You don't mean," Nilly said, his eyes opening wide, "that he actually *has* a vault like that?"

"You wouldn't get in there, no way, little guy," Alfie said. "It's widely considered the world's safest vault. Pick-proof, atomic-bomb-proof, even Crunch-Brother-proof."

"Yup," Betty said. "It will withstand absolutely everything. Impossible to break into. It has infrared and outfrayellow rays that are impossible even for a guy your size to get past."

"Yup," Charlie said. "And even if some invisible ghost who knew all the codes got to it, the inner-most vault has motion detectors that go off the instant the diamond or any of the gold is moved."

"Ugh," Nilly said. "Where is this vault—OW!"

A strong thumb and index finger were pinching one of his ears, lifting him off his seat. The fingers belonged to Mama Crunch, who had just walked in and was now whispering into Nilly's aching ear, "You have very big ears for such a little guy, pipsqueak. *Too* big, if you ask me. And you know what they say: Curiosity killed the cat."

"Do they say that?" Nilly moaned, his eyes brimming with tears from the pain.

"So if you don't want to end up like that cat, maybe you should concentrate on eating."

"Good suggestion, Mrs. Crunch," Nilly said. "Brilliant suggestion, actually."

She let go, and he dropped back down into his chair.

Nilly looked around. It was eerily quiet in the dark room, and he was surrounded by creepily staring eyes.

"Well, well," he said, brushing his hands together.

"Would you look at the time! I think I really ought to thank you for a lovely meal." He hopped down from the chair, walked quickly toward the door, and hoped that no one would yell "Stop" or "Freeze."

"Stop!" Alfie yelled.

"Freeze!" Betty yelled.

Nilly's feet froze on the floor. He wasn't looking forward to whatever was coming next.

"You forgot this."

Nilly slowly turned around and saw that Charlie was holding something out.

"Oh that, yes," Nilly said, grabbing his cigar. "I'll see if I can't manage to set my bed on fire tonight, heh-heh!"

Exactly three seconds later he was out the door.

Her Royal Highness's Even More Secret Service

THE FOG HAD settled like thick pea soup over the streets of London, and Nilly hurried back toward his hotel through the London darkness. The streets and alleys that had been so crowded and lively in the daylight were now a labyrinth, devoid of people, lit only by a few streetlights wearing gray fog hats. And the few sounds Nilly could hear weren't cozy or homey in the least. Trickling and rattling and rustling, the deep sighs of a few drips falling from gutters and eaves and window-sills. Muffled complaints and wailing from behind walls and doors. A sudden, chilling shriek from nowhere.

"Wasn't it here?" he mumbled to himself, and turned left.

Walked a little ways.

"Wasn't it here?" he mumbled, and turned right.

He said this mostly to hear his own voice. And a little to convince himself that he knew where he was, because he had no idea. And the alleys seemed like they were just getting narrower, darker, and more deserted.

"Wasn't it here?" he mumbled again.

"No, it most certainly wasn't."

He was just going to keep on moving when it occurred to him that that last answer hadn't come from him. The voice had come from somewhere just behind him.

Nilly turned around. And a figure in a hat and trench coat stepped out of the darkness.

"Gulp," Nilly said, swiveling back around to run. But a second figure stepped out of the darkness ahead of him. This one was also wearing a hat and a trench coat with an upturned collar. He was surrounded!

"Who—who are you?" Nilly asked, looking for a way out.

"Jack," the first one said. "Jack Jekyll."

"Ripper," the second one said. "Ripper Hyde."

They closed in even more.

"And . . . what you guys want is . . . ," Nilly said, "to, uh . . ."

"We want what you have," Jekyll said, reaching inside his coat for something.

"But—but all I have is a half-chewed wad of gum wrapped up in paper," Nilly said, pressing himself back against the wall. "Or, well, I also have this cigar.

Practically unsmoked. Top of the line. Rolled on the thighs of a beautiful Cuban cigar roller. So I'm awfully reluctant to part with it, hard-core smoker that I am. But go ahead, just take it."

"We mean, we want the information you have," Jekyll said, holding out the thing he'd pulled out of his coat. It was a business card with his picture on it. Next to his name, above the picture—in all caps—it said H.R.H.E.M.S.S.

"We work for Her Royal Highness's Even More Secret Service," Hyde said. "And we've been in touch with our Norwegian colleagues, Helge and Hallgeir. We've been tailing you since you landed in London."

"Oh?" Nilly said, relieved.

"Yes," Jekyll said. "But why are you in this alley? This isn't anywhere near your hotel."

"Oh, that," Nilly said, sticking his cigar in his mouth. "I just wanted to take a little evening stroll to clear my mind." He tapped his finger lightly on his forehead. "And there's a lot of brains up here to clear up, so it takes an extra-long stroll."

"Could we go back to your hotel now and discuss the case?" Jekyll asked.

"Sure," Nilly said.

They stood there looking at one another for a few seconds.

"You can go first," Nilly said.

Then they went.

DOCTOR PROCTOR AND Lisa opened the door, and Nilly introduced them to the two British agents.

"Please forget our names," Jekyll said, taking off his coat. "Just call us Agent One and Agent Two."

"No double *O* in front of that?" Lisa asked.

"Double *O*?" Hyde asked, sounding surprised and adjusting his tie. "Why would there be?"

"No reason," Lisa said. "Are you guys just coming from a wedding?"

"What do you mean?" Jekyll asked.

"Well, you guys are wearing . . . uh, well, tuxedos."

The two men obviously had no idea what she was talking about.

"Let's get started," Hyde said. "What happened?"

They sat down and explained everything. Lisa explained about the money they'd taken from Nilly's Monopoly game and put in the baby carriage, about their disguises, and the mock mugging in the park. And Nilly described fleeing the scene, the bank deposit, and the super-secure bank vault the Crunch Brothers had told him about, where the gold and the diamond were being kept.

"Hmm," Jekyll said, tugging on his handlebar mustache as he listened to Nilly's description of the vault. "There's only one vault in London, well, in the whole world, that has both infrared and outfrayellow rays *and* motion detectors. And that's the vault at the Bank of the Very Rich."

"And where's that?" Doctor Proctor asked.

"Oh, it's not far away," Hyde said.

"More specifically," Jekyll began, and then moved over to the window and pointed, "it's right there."

Everyone else ran over to him. The fog had miraculously just burned off, in typical English fashion, and London lay below them, glittering in the darkness.

"There?" Nilly asked.

"There," Jekyll said.

"Inside Big Ben?" Lisa asked.

"The actual bank is in the Parliament building under the tower," Hyde said. "The government used to meet in that building, but it got bought up and now it's a private bank."

"Someone *bought* the Parliament?" Doctor Proctor asked in his Scottish accent. "Who—"

"Who do you think?" Hyde said. "There's only one person willing to pay whatever it takes to get *exactly* what he wants."

"Rublov," Lisa said. "Maximus Rublov."

"You hit the nail on the head," Jekyll said.

"But . . . why would Rublov agree to store the stolen gold?" Doctor Proctor asked. "It even says Bank of Norway right on the gold bar."

"Elementary, my dear Doctor Proctor," Lisa said. "Maximus Rublov must be behind all the robberies. The Crunch Brothers were working for him."

"But—but what would a rich man like him want with so much money?" Doctor Proctor asked.

"Just as elementary," Lisa said, but then didn't say anything else. She just watched the others as they stood there, scratching their heads.

"Come on, don't be so dim," she said.

"Of course," Doctor Proctor said, smacking himself on the forehead.

"What?" Nilly yelled, hopping up and down impatiently. "What?"

"She means that he needed the extra money to buy that superexpensive soccer player no one could afford to buy," Doctor Proctor said.

"Ibranaldovez," Lisa said.

There were a couple of seconds of silence while everyone let this sink in.

"Okay," Nilly said. "But then we've found the Norwegian gold reserve. Now you secret service guys can just arrest Rublov and go get the Bank of Norway's gold bar back for us."

Jack Jekyll smacked his lips and shook his head. Ripper Hyde shook his head and smacked his lips.

"We can't just arrest a man as important as Rublov without any evidence," Jekyll said.

"Then he'll just buy all of Buckingham Palace and kick out the Queen along with her entire Her Royal Highness's Even More Secret Service," Hyde said.

"Then the Queen would be out of a job, and so would we," Jekyll said.

"Which would mean that, unfortunately, we can't help you," Hyde said.

"Actually, sooner the opposite," Jekyll said, cocking his head and wiggling his eyebrows at Hyde in a funny way. "If you guys are planning to break into the Bank of the Very Rich to take your gold bar back on your own, we're going to have to arrest you."

"Ach, but we dunnae have any plans to—" Doctor Proctor began, but was interrupted by Hyde's unnaturally high voice: "So we'd best be going now before we hear any of you suggest anything like that."

"But if you should happen to find any stolen goods in Rublov's bank vault," Jekyll continued, "of course we would be thrilled. Because then we'd have the evidence we need to put Rublov in jail."

"Before he has a chance to buy Buckingham Palace," Hyde said, putting on his trench coat. A piece of paper sailed out of his pocket and landed on the floor in front of Doctor Proctor.

"Hmm," Jekyll said. "How odd that we happened to bring the floor plans for the bank vault with us, which sadly I've just lost on the floor. What a weird coincidence. You'd almost think we suspected Rublov of these robberies."

"Well, anyway, have a good night," Jekyll said.

"WHAT WAS ALL that about?" Nilly asked after Jekyll and Hyde had gone.

"Don't you get it?" Lisa said. "They want *us* to break into the vault to get them the evidence they need against Rublov."

Doctor Proctor, who had spread out the sheet of paper Jekyll had dropped and was studying the diagrams on it, said, "But I'm afraid that might be very, *very* difficult."

"How difficult?" Lisa asked, her brow furrowed with worry.

"Almost impossible," Doctor Proctor said in a sorrowful voice.

"Yippee!" Nilly said. "Let's get going!"

A Plan Where Absolutely Nothing Can Go Wrong. GUARANTEED. Just Kidding.

THE MOON PEERED down at London as Big Ben chimed heavily three times. And since clockmaker Edward John Dent, who had made the Big Ben clock sometime in 1853, had done a very meticulous job, that meant that the time was now exactly three o'clock in the morning. London was asleep, but the hotel room of our three friends was full of activity.

"What else do you see?" Doctor Proctor asked as he continued to study the diagrams they'd received from Hyde and Jekyll.

"The place is absolutely crawling with guards," said Lisa, who sat with binoculars in front of her eyes. "They're standing around the entire Parliament building and at the entrance to the Big Ben tower. Plus, I've seen them coming and going out of the manhole covers, too. They have stethoscopes around their necks."

"That thing doctors put on your chest to listen and see if your heart is beating the way it's supposed to?" asked Nilly, who was standing on a chair next to Doctor Proctor, looking at the drawings.

"Yes," he answered. "That thing doctors put on your

chest to listen and see if your heart is beating the way it's supposed to. But these guards are using them down in the sewers to listen to see if anyone is trying to dig their way into the vault from below."

"Yup," Lisa said, pointing the binoculars up toward the sky. "And they have floodlights lighting up the airspace over the roof in case anyone tries to break in from above."

"In other words," Doctor Proctor said tiredly, pointing back at the floor plan diagrams to illustrate to Nilly just how impossible it was, "*even if* we were to make it through all three locked, steel-reinforced doors, we still have to get through a room full of laser beams darting back and forth as close together as the strings in a shrimping trawler's nets. And if you break one single beam, then the alarm goes off."

But Nilly wouldn't give in. "You said there's a light switch that turns off the lasers?"

"Yes, but listen to me, Nilly!" Doctor Proctor said,

exhausted, rubbing a hand over his face. "The light switch is *here*, on the wall *behind* all the lasers." He pointed. "You can't get to it without triggering the alarm. They've thought of everything!"

"Hmm," Nilly said, scratching his left sideburn with his right hand. "So if we do make it through there, what's next?"

Doctor Proctor rolled his eyes. "Then you're in the room where the door of the vault is. And motion sensors will detect that you're there and give you thirty seconds to open the door before the alarm goes off."

"Why did they do it like that?" Nilly asked.

"If someone is in there for thirty seconds without being able to open the vault door, then they're probably not supposed to be in there. In other words, a burglar. Right?"

"Clever. And the door and the lock?"

"The door is made of the thickest steel there is, Uddevalla steel. And the combination lock has thirteen numbers and four letters, and the combination changes automatically every hour."

"I see," Nilly said. "But that doesn't sound so hard, does it?"

Doctor Proctor just closed his eyes in response, tilted his head back, and moaned aloud.

"Come on, Doctor, there's a way around everything!" Nilly said. "At least when you're a genius. And you are. Think about it and come up with the perfect bank robbery. Now!"

"If I had four months, maybe. But this has to happen in the next two days if we're going to get the gold back home to Norway in time for the World Bank inspection on Monday! And even if we could pull all that off, which is already impossible, not to mention getting into the vault somehow . . ."

"Yes!" Nilly said. "Great! We're in the vault! What happens then?"

Doctor Proctor blinked. For a second it looked like

he was about to cry. But instead he started laughing like a man who'd finally lost it.

"Don't you remember what Hyde and Jekyll said?" Doctor Proctor finally responded. "The alarm will go off the second the gold or the diamond is moved. And as you can see from the diagrams, there's only one way out. And it leads straight into the arms of Rublov's guards. And where do you suppose the road leads from there?"

"The Crunch Brothers," Lisa said gloomily. "Blood knuckles. Shredded Parmesan cheese."

Nilly didn't look like he was listening. He pointed at the floor plan. "What about this way over here?"

Doctor Proctor leaned over the diagram again. "Sorry, that's just the staircase up into the tower, Nilly. Three hundred and thirty-four steps leading up to the clock. It's just there so the clockmaker can set Big Ben."

"Hmm," Nilly said, scratching his right sideburn with his left hand. "I think I have an idea."

"Oh yes?" Doctor Proctor said.

"Oh no," Lisa said.

"Oh yeah," Nilly said, hopping down off the chair and running over to the hotel window. "We won't make our escape through the front entrance, you see. We'll go up. Up there."

Nilly pointed to the clock face on Big Ben, where the beams of light from the floodlights were sweeping back and forth.

"And how are we going to get away from there?" Lisa asked.

"Not us," Nilly said. "I need to break in alone, because with the mode of transport we're going to be using, there won't be room for anyone besides little old me and the guy flying the getaway craft."

"What kind of craft?" Doctor Proctor asked, puzzled. "And who are you talking about? Who's going to be flying it?"

"I'm talking about a friend of mine who needs to

get out a little more," Nilly said, rubbing his hands together. "I'm going to go call him right now."

"Out of where?" Doctor Proctor asked, still puzzled.

"That little backwater village," Nilly said. "Does anyone know the area code for South Trøndelag?"

"You don't m-m-mean . . . ?" Lisa stammered.

"You don't mean . . . ?" Victor Proctor groaned.

And then in unison they both said, "YOU'RE CRAZY, NILLY!"

The Great
Gold Robbery

THE CLOCK OVER Mr. Stumbleweed's window at the Bank of the Very Rich was exactly—and now I mean exactly—2:16:23:14 p.m., or about a quarter past two, when the front door of the bank opened.

In walked a man dressed in a top hat and an elegant penguin suit—not actually a penguin costume, a tuxedo, but there was something rather penguinlike about it. He was carrying a briefcase that was attached to his wrist. At his side there was a very young, elegantly dressed girl in a sun hat decorated like a fruit plate, except hopefully the fruit was fake. Hopefully the mink stole around her neck was also fake.

They walked right up to the window where Mr. Stumbleweed was sitting and asked him if they could rent a safety-deposit box. Mr. Stumbleweed explained the hair-raising sum the bank charged annually for a safety-deposit box, and they listened without fainting or protesting. Then he and two armed guards escorted the two new customers down to the basement. There Mr. Stumbleweed unlocked not just one but three locked steel doors, and then they were standing in the safety-deposit room. The safety-deposit boxes were the size of shoe boxes stacked on their sides, and they covered two of the walls in the room.

"No one without authorization can gain access to

this room," Mr. Stumbleweed said with satisfaction. "And of course we promise complete discretion. Neither we nor anyone else will know what valuables you store in your box."

"Nice to know yur bank is secure," the new customer said in his pronounced Scottish accent. "But tell me, aren't we almost in the inner sanctum here?"

"I assume you mean the bank vault, Doctor MacKaroni," Mr. Stumbleweed said with a smile. "Well, you're part of the way in, but you still need to get through the laser beams, the motion detectors, and a door made of authentic Uddevalla steel. Well, you would have to get through those if you and your niece were planning to break in, I mean," Mr. Stumbleweed said with a sniveling laugh, to which the two new clients responded with a smile and a polite nod.

"Then we'll give you bank box sixty-seven," Mr. Stumbleweed said, and handed Doctor MacKaroni two keys. "One primary key and one reserve key. If you'd like to put anything in your box now, the guards and I will wait outside until you're done."

"Thank you," Doctor MacKaroni said.

As Mr. Stumbleweed waited outside the reinforced door, he heard Doctor MacKaroni's briefcase being opened and closed and then the door of the safety-deposit box being locked again. He had to admit that occasionally he was curious and wished he could sneak a peek at what the customers put in their safety-deposit boxes. Diamonds? Gold? Their wills? Secret love letters? But it was none of his business. So when Doctor MacKaroni came out again with a briefcase that seemed a good deal lighter, naturally Mr. Stumbleweed didn't ask any questions. Although there was no rule against thinking about it. And in his head, Mr. Stumbleweed guessed jewelry. Maybe the family's heirlooms: emeralds, rubies, opals, and other expensive baubles.

When the two left the bank, the clock over Mr. Stumbleweed's window said 2:34:41:09 p.m., or a little after two thirty.

NILLY WOKE UP and stretched. Which is to say, he tried to stretch, but it wasn't so easy to accomplish where he was. He twisted and looked at the numbers on his watch glowing in the silent darkness: 2:40 p.m. In other words, a little more after two thirty. It was time to get to work. But getting up wasn't exactly easy. He was lying scrunched up in something that wasn't much bigger than a shoe box, and one of his feet had fallen asleep. He fumbled around underneath him with his hand until he found what he was looking for. One of the keys, the reserve key, to the safety-deposit box. He managed to stick it into the keyhole from the inside, twisted it, and opened it cautiously. Then he squeezed his body out the opening. Once he was free, he jumped. He tried to land softly, but he'd forgotten that one of his feet was asleep, so he ended up collapsing onto the concrete floor.

He lay there for a bit, looking up at the open safety-deposit box above him. And he thought that every once in a while—*once in a while*—it wasn't so bad to be the smallest boy anyone had ever seen.

He stood up, but his foot was still asleep and was like limp spaghetti under him, so he had to sit back down. He looked at his watch again. 2:43. He had exactly seventeen minutes until the appointed time. He pulled a little bottle out of his pocket: DOCTOR PROCTOR'S FROST FLUID. He opened the bottle and downed the contents. Then he made a face and reminded himself to ask the professor to add a little more sugar next time.

Then he stood up again, and this time his foot held him, if only just barely.

He turned right down the hallway the way they'd planned, and sure enough: The hallway turned twice to the left and then once to the right, just like in the diagram. He heard a whirring noise that was steadily getting louder, and he realized he was getting closer. And there—at the end of the hallway—he saw something on the wall that looked like a normal light switch. But he knew it wasn't. Nilly stopped suddenly. Even though he couldn't see anything, just an empty hallway, he knew that there, right in front of him, lurked an invisible threat. Nilly took out the cigar he'd gotten from Alfie Crunch, lit it with the lighter he'd gotten from Doctor Proctor, and steeled himself. Then he inhaled the smoke and exhaled quickly and vigorously, straight in front of him.

And then he could see them.

The laser beams.

He inhaled and exhaled several more times, until the space in front of him was full of smoke and he could see the whole pattern the beams made. They were coming from the walls, the floor, and the ceiling and formed a thorny thicket so thick and dense that it would be impossible for even the smallest boy anyone had ever seen to make it through without touching one of the beams. He could only just barely see the switch on the other side through the web of laser beams.

But there *was* a tiny little opening there.

Nilly checked his watch. Fourteen minutes left. He plunged his hand down into his other pants pocket and pulled up the blue aiming mitten and the three darts, put on the mitten, and aimed through the opening.

He threw.

THUNK!

The dart made it through the thicket but missed the switch by half an inch.

Nilly grabbed dart number two.

It was not particularly warm in the bank basement, and yet he felt sweat trickling down his back. The dart was trembling in his hand.

"Come on, Nilly," he whispered to himself, and threw.

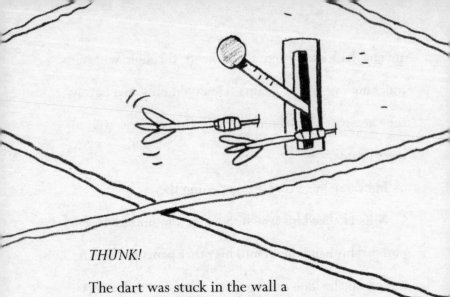

THUNK!

The dart was stuck in the wall a

hairbreadth from the switch, vibrating. But it had

bumped the first dart as it went in, and Nilly could see

the yellow end of that first dart slowly starting to sag.

It was going to fall out of the wall! And if it did that,

it would hit one of the laser beams, which ran right

under the switch!

Nilly grabbed the third and final black dart and

didn't even have time to aim. He just threw it as fast

as he could. The yellow dart came loose from the wall

right then. Nilly followed it with his eyes. It felt like it

was falling in slow motion. Toward the beam below.

And it *hit* the beam.

At least, it hit where the laser beam *used* to be.

Then it hit the floor.

Nilly stood there staring straight ahead.

The laser beams were gone.

And the black dart was stuck in the middle of the switch, quivering.

Nilly wiped a hand across his sweaty forehead and looked at the clock. Thirteen minutes. Then he started running again.

THIS IS SO exciting it must seem like complete idiocy to end the chapter here, but that's exactly what I was planning on doing.

The Great Escape

BACK SO SOON?

Okay, so Nilly made it past the laser beams, which he had managed to turn off, and ran into the room in front of the world's most secure vault with the door made of authentic Uddevalla steel and a lock with a combination that was thirteen numbers and four letters long.

And as he entered the room, he noticed a clock on the wall that had already begun to count down. He knew that the motion detectors had detected him and that if he didn't open the steel door within thirty seconds, the system would decide he was a burglar—which would actually be a completely correct assumption. Then the alarm would go off. In twenty-seven more seconds. Twenty-six . . .

Nilly knew there was no way he could correctly guess thirteen numbers and four letters. So instead he unbuttoned his pants and aimed at the lock on the steel door. According to Doctor Proctor, the ice-blue frost fluid took only three minutes to blend with your stomach acid and pass through your liver, spleen, kidneys, and other innards before it was ready to be peed out. Nilly strained, trying to start the flow.

Twenty seconds.

"Come on," he mumbled.

Sixteen seconds.

He pushed harder, groaned. But it's not always so easy to pee when you know that you *have to*.

Nilly had heard that it helps to think about running water when you're pee shy. So he thought about a trickling faucet, rainwater burbling out of a downspout, a babbling spring stream. But nothing came.

Twelve seconds.

An average-sized river. A big river. A waterfall. Nine seconds. Niagara, Vøringsfossen, and Victoria Falls all in one.

Seven seconds. Something had to happen. ASAP.

"Okay, reverse psychology," Nilly muttered to himself, closing his eyes and thinking as hard as he could about how he absolutely *couldn't* pee, not here in a public place, not inside the Bank of the Very Rich.

Four seconds.

What a scandal that would be! He would be the laughingstock in the newspapers. Headline: BOY PEES ON

WORLD'S MOST SECURE STEEL DOOR. MAYOR OF UDDEVALLA FURIOUS!

A yellow beam, straight as a laser beam, squirted forth, hitting the steel door and the lock.

Nilly didn't dare look up at the clock; he just peed as fast as he could. The beam stopped, and he raised the foot with the wood-chopping shoe and kicked the lock.

It sounded like falling icicles crashing onto a sidewalk, the tinkling, singing, crashing, crushing sound of something shattering into a thousand pieces.

Nilly grabbed the handle on the iron door and pulled it toward himself.

It had to open!

It *did* open.

Nilly glanced up at the clock on the wall. It had stopped at 0.5 seconds.

He shuddered and pulled the door open wide.

He saw exactly what he'd been hoping to see.

The vault contained a pile of gold bars glittering

dimly in the light from the doorway. And there was a gigantic diamond the size of a soccer ball on top of the pile, sparkling like a disco ball.

Nilly looked at his watch. He had eleven minutes to find the Bank of Norway's gold bar and get out of there.

He hurried into the vault and was about to move the diamond when he remembered that he couldn't touch anything, that that would trigger the alarm right away. So instead he squatted down and read what it said on the gold bars that he could see in the pile.

Banco Central do Brasil. Banco Central do Brasil. Banco Central do Brasil. Banco Central do . . . What if the gold bar from the Bank of Norway was somewhere in the middle of the pile and he couldn't find it? Should he just grab one of Brazil's gold bars instead? Nilly listened to the voices inside his head. His mother's voice said, "What difference would it make? Gold is gold, and Brazil obviously has plenty." And Lisa's said,

"No, Nilly! Taking from others is stealing, no matter how desperate you are!"

Nilly looked at his watch again. Six minutes to three. He hated clocks!

But then he saw something! It was partially hidden in the pile, but some of the letters were visible. ——NK OF N—— something. The next letter looked curvy. Probably an *O*. He wanted to fling aside the gold bars that were in the way, but he knew the guards would be there a few seconds after the alarm went off, so he had to be completely sure he had the right bar first. ——NK OF NO—— That couldn't be anything other than the Bank of Norway. Or could it?

Nilly started rattling off countries as fast as he could. However, the only "NO" possibilities were Northern Cyprus, North Korea, Norfolk Island, Northern Marianas, or Norway. And of those, only North Korea and Norway had their own currencies. Which meant his chances were quite good that it said BANK OF NORWAY on it.

He stood up. It was two and a half minutes to three. He had an appointment at three o'clock, and if Doctor Proctor hadn't made any mistakes when he estimated how long it would take Nilly from here, now was the perfect time for him to get going!

As Nilly pushed the first gold bar aside, he heard the alarm start screeching. Yowzers, gold was really heavy! He knocked two gold bars off and picked up the one he'd seen. And let out a little "Yippee!" because, sure enough: It said BANK OF NORWAY on the side. Nilly stuffed the gold bar down into the little sack he had on his back and ran out of the vault. He ran back the same way he'd come, but when he passed the room with the safety-deposit boxes and the three steel doors, he turned left instead of right and came to a door that wasn't made of steel, but of normal wood. It said CLOCK TOWER. Nilly could hear shouts and boots running, clattering and rattling down the stairs from the bank offices up above.

Nilly raised the wood-chopping shoe and kicked fast and furiously so that the door was quickly a pile of shavings and bits of wood. Then he started running up the stairs as fast as those tiny legs could carry the little boy with the heavy gold bar.

Three hundred thirty-four steps, Doctor Proctor had said. It hadn't sounded like all that many when they'd discussed it in the hotel room, but if he was going to make it, he needed to cover at least two steps a second! His thighs were burning and the stairs seemed like they would never end, but Nilly didn't give up. Upward, upward, around in circles, ever higher.

And when the steps did finally end, he found himself on a landing with a bunch of gears of all possible sizes, which were whirring and spinning and ticking and tocking. Nilly found the little hatch in the wall he was looking for, opened it, and leaned out.

The wind hit his face.

"Ho, ho!" he said with a smile.

Because when he looked down, he saw little ants running back and forth and gesturing and screaming down below. And when he looked across at the other side of the Thames, he saw the sun gleaming in a window that he knew was the window of the hotel room where Doctor Proctor and Lisa, elegantly dressed in a penguin jacket and faux mink stole, were watching him through the binoculars. Then he looked up at the blue sky, where the contraption that had flown almost to Denmark would soon come to snatch him up, right under the snouts of Rublov's dogs. Come fly away with the world's best, bravest, most brazen, and most attractive bank robber! Nilly looked down. He hoped the news that the Bank of the Very Rich was being robbed had spread and that the TV cameras would be in place quickly enough to witness the Great Escape.

Nilly crawled out the hatch and onto the hour hand of Big Ben, which was right below the hatch, pointing horizontally to the number three. Lisa had been the one to realize that it would be best to plan the escape for exactly three o'clock so that Nilly could safely stand on the hour hand, which would be straight out.

Nilly scanned the sky. He should have been able to spot Petter by now, since he could already hear the footsteps approaching up the stairs. "Come on, Petter!" Nilly muttered to himself. "Come on!"

Just then he felt something vibrate in his pocket. He pulled out his cell phone.

"Nilly here."

"Hi, it's Petter."

Nilly gulped. "Do not tell me you're calling to say you're running a little late, Petter."

"No, no."

"Good!" Nilly said, relieved.

"No, I'm not going to be a *little* bit late. I'm going to be *very* late."

"What?!" Nilly shouted. "What's up?"

"You know, England, rain, stuff like that."

"Rain? The weather is lovely here!" Nilly cried.

"I had a headwind coming over the North Sea, see. And rain when I reached the English coastline. The hang glider was soaking wet, and I . . . I guess I've been going a little heavy on the hot chocolate lately. I've just gained a little too much weight, Nilly."

"You're—you're not going to make it?" Nilly groaned.

"I landed in a field and there's not a soul around, and—"

Just then Big Ben began to strike, drowning out the rest of what Petter said. It reverberated, thundered, and throbbed, and the short hand vibrated. This all happened so quickly that Nilly lost his balance and fell forward. He flung up his arms in desperation, and his tiny fingers managed to grasp hold of the hour hand. He was only just barely hanging on. He looked down and saw his cell phone falling and falling some more, down toward the human ants and the toy cars way below, and

he didn't feel like yelling "Ho, ho!" anymore. Nor did he want to know how far it was to the ground, but Lisa had told him: ninety-six meters. Which, if you want to know, is three hundred and fifteen feet.

Nilly's fingers were already starting to lose their grasp on the hour hand. Nilly was certainly a rather strong little boy, but with the heavy gold bar in the sack on his back and his fingers getting sweatier and sweatier, how was this going to go? I'm just asking, you know?

A Cow, a Mirage, and the Great Interrogation

"HELLO?!" PETTER YELLED into the phone.

It sounded like it was really windy on Nilly's end of the line. Then there was a loud crash.

"Nilly?!" Petter yelled.

But now there was only silence on the other end of the line. And then a dial tone.

Dejected, Petter stuck his phone back in his pocket and looked around. But his glasses were so fogged up from the rain that he couldn't see much. So he took them off and determined that he was still in a deserted, rain-soaked field somewhere in the British countryside. He hadn't seen a place this deserted since . . . well, since he'd left Norway at dawn.

Nilly, Lisa, and Doctor Proctor had called Petter last night. They'd given him thorough instructions on how to fly to Big Ben in London and pick Nilly up from the hour hand at exactly three o'clock. Petter hadn't found out any more than that, well, aside from Nilly saying something about the gross domestic gold reserve and it being important.

Petter tugged the waistband of his underwear up—it was the only article of clothing that still had any dry patches left on it—and wiped his eyeglasses. Then he put his glasses on and looked around. Now he could see a little more, not that what he saw was any more encouraging. A hang glider that was as soaking wet as he was, an equally soaking-wet cow chewing its cud and looking bored to death. Plus a mirage that was slogging toward him. The mirage was of a woman in a red tracksuit, not unlike his own suit, originally intended for cross-country skiing. The mirage slowly got bigger and bigger. Until it obviously thought it was big enough and stopped, right in front of Petter. And it must have been quite a mirage, because—go figure— it started talking to him too.

"How do you do?" it said.

Petter stared. The mirage looked like a woman around his age with wet, stringy hair and glasses with the thickest lenses he'd ever seen. On a woman.

"I—I—" Petter said, surprised to find himself talking back to the mirage! "I'm Petter. I'm the one and only Petter. Who are you?"

"I'm Petronella. Is this your hang glider?"

Petter squinted one eye shut and looked at the

woman named Petronella. He nodded that this was indeed his hang glider. "Yes. I sell dem."

"Really? I like hang gliders. And I'm in sales too. Old Hillman cars," the mirage said, pointing.

The wisps of fog had thinned a bit, and Petter saw a farm building on top of a hill. In front of the house he saw the contours of the old used cars for sale.

"Sell you very many?" Petter asked.

"There's no one left to sell to. Everybody's moved to the city," she said, shaking her head. "It's only me left here."

Petter nodded. Tell him about it. He knew how it was.

"Would you care for some tea?" the mirage asked.

"Vaht?" Petter asked.

"Would you like some tea?"

"Oh," Petter said when he finally understood her English. "You have some hot chocolate, do you?"

The mirage who called herself Petronella lit up in

a big smile. "You prefer hot chocolate to tea, then, too?"

Petter nodded slowly. This had to be a mirage. A woman who liked hang gliders *and* hot chocolate—it was simply too good to be true. If it turned out she liked to play Chinese checkers too—ha-ha!—well then, he would know for sure he was dreaming.

"Come on, let's go make some hot chocolate," she said, holding out the palest hand Petter had ever seen. So pale it was almost transparent. But it *was* a hand. She was no mirage. Because now he was holding it. And he felt absolutely no desire to ever let go of this hand. A wonderful thought hit him. That maybe this was the most successful unsuccessful landing in his entire hang-gliding life.

And with that the two of them strolled across the field toward the farmhouse and the rusty Hillman cars at the top of the hill. And then Petter had the thought that Nilly had probably been exaggerating—

surely picking him up off that behemoth of a clock in London couldn't be *that* important.

I'M GOING TO die, Nilly thought. *I'm going to die because of England's lousy weather and a slightly overweight dude from South Trøndelag.*

He twitched, but his hands and feet were bound too tightly to the chair he was sitting in.

The reason Nilly was so sure he was going to die was that the little man in front of him had just said so. "You're going to die," the man had said. And he had sounded rather convincing.

Nilly stared at the man's familiar face. Familiar because Nilly had a mask that looked just like it. Prominent forehead, receding hairline, and narrow, painfully precisely trimmed eyebrows and goatee. Maximus Rublov in the diminutive flesh.

And behind him, on the sofa in the dim light of the Crunch family's living room, sat the Crunch Brothers, staring at him with cold, accusatory looks. And then behind them, with her arms crossed, stood she whose name people only just barely dare to whisper.

"Kill me here, kill me there," Nilly said. "If you really wanted me dead, why'd you save me from Big Ben? Two more seconds and I would have lost my grip and you would've been spared all this killing and I would have been spared these ropes and you would've been spared tying them and——"

"Quiet!" Rublov screamed so the blackout curtains fluttered. "My guards saved you for two simple reasons, you freckled pygmy! First of all, because you had a gold bar in your backpack. And second of all, because before you die you're going to tell me who else was in on this robbery."

"Who else?" Nilly said with as scornful a laugh as he could muster. "I don't trust any other robbers, Mr. Rublov. I work alone."

Rublov crossed his arms and ran a gloved finger thoughtfully over his lips. "Are you really even a robber, Mr. Sherl? If that's even your real name. Are you sure you don't work for Scotland Yard? Or Her Royal Highness's Even More Secret Service?"

"The police?" Nilly said, laughing so hard he felt the fillings in his molars clacking together. "I hardly think a career in police work would be a good fit for a master thief. . . ."

"Quiet! You're going to die anyway. The only choice you have is whether it will be a pain-free death or"—Rublov smiled wanly—"death by blood knuckles."

Nilly gulped. Dread and horror, he'd be shredded like Parmesan if he didn't talk! If only he were wearing his wood-chopping shoe. But they'd removed it when they captured him. Now it was sitting on the coffee table along with his aiming mitten, the darts, and the bottle containing the rest of Doctor Proctor's Frost Fluid.

Rublov came all the way up to Nilly's chair and lowered his voice. "Or were you perhaps stealing the gold for someone who wants to buy Ibranaldovez right out from under my nose? If so, you lose, you little barn gnome, because the purchase will be final as of five o'clock tonight. The gold was all dispatched from the vault an hour ago. So you might as well give up and tell me everything."

"So Lisa was right. That's what you needed all that

money for," Nilly said. "To buy the world's best soccer player before Saturday's final World Cup game."

"I don't know who this Lisa person is, but let me put it this way," Rublov said, sneering so his sharp, wet teeth gleamed. "The Rotten Ham team had hardly a microchance of beating us before we had the world's best player on our team. Now they have even less of one." Rublov laughed a wheezy, high-pitched laugh.

"But why are you willing to pay so much just to win a—a soccer game?"

"Surely someone like you must understand that, Sherl," Rublov said, raising one of his overly pruned eyebrows.

"Someone like me?" Nilly asked.

"Yes. You were teased in school for being small too, weren't you?"

"Yeah, sure," Nilly said, contemplating that for a moment.

"Well then, I'm sure you can imagine how I felt

when my dad sent me from Moscow to England to a ridiculously expensive boarding school for upper-class boys? My father thought it would teach me to act like a proper rich person, so I'd be ready to inherit all his money someday. But all I learned there was to hate those confounded snobs who made fun of me because I wasn't just like them!"

"Yes, well, I suppose we're both in a bad situation, Maximus," Nilly said with a sigh. "But maybe especially me, since I'm about to die. So what do you say you just untie me and——"

"Shh," Maximus said, staring stiffly straight ahead, and then continued, his voice trembling with emotion. "They wouldn't let me play on the soccer team at school because I was on the short side."

"Surely it was because you weren't particularly good——" Nilly began.

"Silence! But now they can sit in their trite upper-class homes with their disgruntled wives and children and watch who's going to win the World Cup! Who's the best *now*, huh?" Rublov moved his silver-plated cane up to touch the bottom of Nilly's chin. "Who, Sherl? Say it!"

"Uh . . . Ibranaldovez?" Nilly said.

"You idiot! The *owner* of the team is the best! That's me, Sherl! Maximus Rublov!"

"Let's say that's the case," Nilly said, giving a tug to see if the rope he was tied up with had loosened at all. It hadn't. He sighed again. "But have you actually given any thought to what's going to happen when the police find the gold bars and discover that you used them to buy Ibranaldovez? It actually says right on the bars where they come from, and that will prove that you stole them."

"Of course I've thought of that, you turnip! No one will ever see where the gold came from, because I melted it down!"

"Mel-melted it down?" Nilly said with a gulp.

"Of course! All those Brazilian gold bars have been turned into gold coins like this one." Rublov proudly pulled a coin out of his trouser pocket and held it up in front of Nilly. It bore Maximus Rublov's chinless profile and the text 1 RUBLOV.

"I'm going to pay for Ibranaldovez with these coins. The whole world will be using this currency in a few years, Nilly. All I have to do is buy enough countries first. Norway is obviously at the top of my shopping list."

"You're planning to *buy* Norway?"

"Oh yes. Buying a country is easier than you think. And Norway won't cost very much once the World Bank finds out you guys don't have any gold reserve anymore. And do you know what I'm planning to buy Norway with? The very same gold bar I stole from you Norwegians!" Rublov laughed his loud, squealing laugh again. "Isn't that amusingly ingenious?"

"So you melted our gold bar into coins too?"

"No," Rublov said. "That's the unusual thing. The coin maker said there was too much carbosidium nitrate phosphate in the Norwegian gold."

"And what is carbo . . . ?" Nilly asked.

"No idea. But apparently it means the coins would come out too soft, kind of like chocolate coins. So we sent the gold to another goldsmith, who's remelting your gold bar right now—"

"Oh NO!"

"Oh yes! And this isn't just any old goldsmith. It's the woman who's making the World Cup trophy that the winning team will be awarded after the final game on Saturday. Don't you see? This is ultra-ingenious! If the police ransack my house looking for gold bars, they'll just find a gold trophy, which they will know that I won fair and square by thoroughly trouncing Rotten Ham. Mwa-ah-ah!"

"Maximus Rublov, I hereby declare you mentally unstable," Nilly said, shaking his head.

"I am *not* mentally unstable!" Rublov hissed.

"Oh, you're not?" Nilly said. "Well, if you've got such a great plan, then you don't need me to tell you anything at all."

Rublov scratched his extremely neatly trimmed goatee. "You know what, Sherl? By golly, you're not so dumb after all. Because that's entirely right: I will be just fine without any information from you at all."

"Great!" Nilly said. "Then maybe I could just go? I'm supposed to meet someone at the movies and—"

"Go?" Rublov grinned widely. "What do you say, you wretched unwashed masses?" He turned to look at the Crunch family. "Should we let the puny one go?"

"Mwa-ah-ah!" they all responded in chorus.

"I thought as much," Rublov said, grabbing his hat and coat. "I have to go, but I'm leaving you in the hands of"—he lowered his voice to a whisper—"Mama Crunch."

Then the door banged shut behind him, and the

dragon mother stepped forward. She breathed her rotten food breath on Nilly and pinched his cheek between her thumb and index finger and said, "So, you thought you could trick Mama by lavishing praise on her pudding, huh? You miserable little meat scrap of an extremely pathetic person! I'm going to the store now to buy spaghetti. That's the boys' absolute favorite. Spaghetti with what, do you suppose?"

"P-p-parmesan cheese?" Nilly guessed, his teeth chattering in his mouth.

"Correct, Mr. Sherl. So get ready to play . . ." She swung her hand out in a sweeping gesture toward the sofa so her upper arm fat swayed and wobbled, and all three of her sons replied in unison, "BLOOD KNUCKLES!"

The Blood
Knuckle Battle.
Sorry: The BIG Blood
Knuckle Battle

"IT'S NO USE," Doctor Proctor groaned, looking at the clock. "We've been searching London for four hours, and our wee Nilly is nowhere to be found."

"But he has to be somewhere," Lisa said with determination.

It was starting to get dark, and Lisa and Doctor Proctor had gone back to the square where they'd started. It was easy to recognize, because there was a column in the middle of the square that was so tall it was impossible to see who the statue on top was of, but Doctor Proctor said it was some guy named Nilsen or Nelson or something, not the host of *Norway's Biggest Liar* but some moderately famous sailor.

"As long as Nilly's alive," Lisa whispered, and the professor saw a tear in the corner of her eye.

"I notified Scotland Yard. They're out looking for him too," Doctor Proctor said. "You'll see."

"And to think I was jealous of Nilly!" Lisa whispered.

"You were?" Doctor Proctor asked. "Why?"

"Because I never get to do the zany stuff. I always have to be the proper, sensible one who has to look after Nilly and be careful. I want to be zany and have fun and have the whole world looking at me!"

"But Lisa, without you we would never have been able to do all the things we've accomplished together."

"Without me," Lisa sniffed, "Nilly wouldn't be a prisoner wherever he is, where he's going to die! Just because I was jealous and didn't want him to be such a huge success *every* time!"

"Hmm," Doctor Proctor said. "And now you're feeling guilty because you think your wish has come true?"

"Yes!" Lisa said, and began bawling.

"And you think that makes you a bad person? Perhaps you think our wee Nilly was never jealous of you for anything?"

"Me?" Lisa said, wiping her tears away with her jacket sleeve. "What's there to be jealous of *me* for?"

"I wonder if our wee Nilly wouldn't like parents like yours, to be someone everyone thinks is cute and all that. And to be clever and self-confident the way you are."

"Self-confident? I'm not—"

"Oh, yes you are." Doctor Proctor took off his swim goggles and wiped the fog out of them. "You just have the type of self-confidence that's unobtrusive and doesn't grab the spotlight so much. But it's all the stronger for that, lassie. And you'll discover that for yourself eventually."

"I will?"

"I promise." Victor Proctor put his goggles back on and patted her head. "And remember that you two love each other more than you're jealous of each other."

"Yes," Lisa said emphatically, "we do!"

Doctor Proctor nodded. "Now let's get back to our hotel and have something to eat and take a little rest."

"Then we have to search some more!" Lisa said, now finished drying her tears. "Do you think he's—"

"Nilly will be fine," Doctor Proctor said, trying his best to give Lisa a reassuring smile. "That boy always has an ace up his sleeve."

ALFIE CRUNCH SHUFFLED the cards slowly, smiling menacingly at Nilly the whole time.

"Have you ever wondered why Parmesan cheese smells like smelly feet, small fry?" Alfie asked as he started dealing out the cards to Betty, Charlie, Nilly, and himself.

"No," Nilly said, gleefully dangling his legs and hands from his chair. Sure, he was going to die, but at least he wasn't tied up anymore. And who knows—maybe blood knuckles wouldn't be as rough as everyone made it sound.

"It's because Parmesan is made out of people who've lost at blood knuckles," Charlie said. "They get so scared they start sweating, especially their toes, which are the last part to be chopped up."

"It smells like stinky feet because it *is* stinky feet," Betty said with a snigger.

"Just as well that people don't know what they're

putting on their spaghetti," Alfie said, looking at his cards with satisfaction. "But lately some of the restaurants we sell to have said that our Parmesan smells *too much* like toe cheese. So we've been thinking about starting to let our victims use these." He pointed to a bunch of fabric eye masks sitting in the bowler hat on the table. BRITISH AIRWAYS was printed in white on each of them. "Actually, they're for covering your eyes when you try to sleep on airplanes and stuff. We snagged them in business class on our flight home from our bank robbery in Brazil. If the victims don't have to watch themselves being turned into Parmesan cheese, their feet won't sweat as much, right?"

"Su-su-supersmart," Nilly said, looking down at his cards. Three of diamonds, five of clubs, eight of spades, ten of hearts, and a jack of diamonds that stared mournfully back at him. He had nothing. His knuckles hurt already.

"So how much are you putting in, pipsqueak?" Alfie asked.

"Nuh-nuh-nothing," Nilly said. "I fold."

"You have to ante up, and the minimum bet is five," Charlie said.

"Then I guess I'll put in," Nilly said reluctantly, scratching at his sideburn, "five."

"All right, let's show our hands," Alfie said.

Everyone laid their cards on the table. Charlie had a pair of nines. Alfie had a pair of fours. And Betty had nothing, just like Nilly.

"That's five blows to you, pipsqueak," Alfie said.

"That's cheating!" Nilly said.

Alfie lowered his unibrow so it ran straight over his pair of angry eyes like a rain gutter. "You're not accusing an Englishman of not playing fair, are you, little guy?"

"Betty's hand is as bad as mine!" Nilly protested.

"So what? We're playing against you as a team. You have to beat all three of us. Those are the rules, and it's not like anyone here got any extra cards. We all got five. So don't say it's not fair. Present your knuckles, you dwarf broccoli!"

Nilly held out a trembling hand with his fist clenched. "C-c-can I wear that eye mask?"

"Not for just five blows, you weakling!" Alfie said, grabbing the deck of cards and rapping Nilly soundly on the knuckles with it. One, two, three, four, five times.

"Ow, ow, ow, ow, ow," Nilly said, pulling back his hand.

It really hurt, and his knuckles were red already.

"Aw, no way. The little guy looks like he's gonna cry," Alfie said with a sneer. "Should we call Mama Crunch and ask if she can bring you a little Birmingham pudding to make you feel better?"

"Heh-heh!" Betty laughed.

"Heh-*cough!*-heh," Charlie laughed.

Nilly blinked and blinked, but the tears wouldn't go away. "It's not fair!" he said, his voice sounding like he was on the verge of tears. "You're not playing by the official international rules of blood knuckles!"

"What rules?" Alfie asked with a disparaging sniff.

"Well, for example, the rule that says you have to hit with the cards faceup!" Nilly said, wiping his eyes with his sleeve as Alfie dealt the next round. "Of course, that's a lot more painful. But no, that's just so typically English. You guys have to do everything differently: drive on the wrong side, use yards instead of meters, spell everything funny, don't speak any foreign languages. . . ."

"Shut up and play!" Alfie barked. "The minimum wager doubles each time, so now it's ten."

"Ten," Nilly said, and then spread his cards out on the table.

"You have a pair of tens?" Alfie said. "Not bad."

"Ha!" Betty said, showing his three kings.

Nilly stuck out his right fist, and Alfie raised the deck of cards. Then reconsidered. Then grunted and rotated the deck so the cards were faceup and then smacked Nilly's knuckles with them.

"Ow!" Nilly yelled. And then, "Double ow!" And then, so loud the porcelain plate on the wall with the picture of the crown prince and princess shook: "Owwwwww!"

"Sounds like the little guy was right!" Charlie cried, plugging his ears. "It really does hurt a lot more if you follow the international rules!"

"Awesome," Alfie said, really laying into it on the last blow, drawing a trickle of blood from two of Nilly's knuckles. "Let's play by the international rules from now on!"

He shuffled and dealt again while Nilly wiped away more tears and blew on his knuckles.

"Hah!" Betty said when he saw his cards.

"Yes!" Charlie said when he saw his cards.

"Would you look at that?" Alfie crowed when he saw his.

"Jackpots poker," Nilly said.

"Huh?" the brothers all said in unison, looking at him.

"I bet a thousand blows and I say, jackpots poker!"

"A thousand blows and what poker?"

"Jackpots poker," Nilly said. "That means that we deal the cards again, but the pot stays and you have to have at least a pair of jacks to continue. Anyone who can't keep going gets fifty blows to the knuckles."

"I don't want fifty blows to the knuckles," Betty said.

"Me either!" Charlie said with a shudder.

"Good," Nilly said. "Then you guys are all in. Deal the cards again, Alfie."

"No way, I like my hand!" Alfie said.

"You were the one who said that from now on we were going to play by the international rules and that Englishmen always play honestly," Nilly said.

Alfie stared at Nilly for a few seconds, furious, then muttered something under his breath, gathered all the cards, and shuffled them again. Then dealt a new round.

"I bet two thousand blows," Nilly said after he'd looked at his cards. "And I say *jackpots*."

The brothers groaned.

After six rounds of jackpots like this, Alfie was really mad. "Enough messing around! There's ten thousand blows in the pot, and that means the loser is going to be Parmesan cheese not just once, but three times over! So this was the last round of jackpots. Now let's PLAY! All right?"

The brothers watched as the little redheaded boy shrugged and said, "Fine by me."

Alfie carefully shuffled the cards, keeping his eye on Nilly. "You haven't been complaining that you got a bad hand each time, pipsqueak. You should have been. Most of the people we play against accuse me of rigging the cards."

"Never occurred to me," Nilly said, taking his cards. "I raise my bet by ten thousand more blows. Anyone in?"

"Me!" the brothers all cried in unison.

Betty was the first to show his cards: a pair of threes.

Alfie rolled his eyes and showed three jacks. "Three of a kind, jacks!" he bragged.

"Good, but not good enough!" Charlie said jubilantly, slapping his cards onto the table. A six, a seven, an eight, a nine, and a ten. "A five-card straight beats three of a kind! Ha-ha!"

The brothers turned and stared tensely at Nilly. Although now that you mention it, Alfie, who had dealt the cards, didn't really look that tense. But he was even more surprised than the other two when Nilly flung both arms up in the air and shouted, "I win!"

"Impossible," Alfie hissed. "Let me see your cards, you little rhubarb."

Nilly laid his cards down on the table. For a couple of seconds it was completely quiet in the room. Then first

Alfie began to laugh, then Betty, and finally Charlie.

"You just have a pair of twos!" Betty said.

"Plus a three of clubs," Nilly said with satisfaction. "And the queen of hearts!"

"That doesn't help. You're last!" Charlie said.

"You're Parmesan cheese," Alfie said.

"No way," Nilly said.

"No way?"

"You guys are forgetting that we're playing by the international rules, boys."

"So what?" Alfie said.

"Since you guys are authentic competitive international poker players, I'm sure you know the rules," Nilly said, pointing to Charlie's cards. "First of all, it doesn't count as a straight when the cards go *up*, like from six to ten. According to paragraph nineteen, an approved straight has to go *down*, like from six to two, for example."

"Darn it!" Charlie said, scratching his head.

"Besides," Nilly said, physically whacking Betty's pair of threes with his own three of clubs, chanting victoriously, "three of clubs! Three of clubs."

"Huh?" Betty said. "What are you doing?"

"Exactly what it says on my card. Clubbing your pair of threes. If you club a pair of threes, you knock them down to half size, making them one and a half. Which means my pair of twos beats your pair of one and a halves. Simple math!"

"You're smart, pipsqueak," Alfie said. "But that doesn't help, because I have three jacks!"

Nilly triumphantly held up his queen of hearts and waved it tauntingly.

"What about it?" Alfie grumbled.

"I trump you with the queen of hearts. Because she's the mother of those three jacks. And she says it's time for her three little jacks to go to bed now."

"What a bunch of nonsense!" Alfie said, standing up.

"Oh yeah?" Nilly said. "Do you guys want me to

tell"—he lowered his voice—"Mama Crunch"—he raised his voice again—"that her boys disrespected the queen of hearts? And that they're *cheating* at blood knuckles?"

Complete silence filled the room for exactly six and a half seconds.

Then Alfie Crunch lowered his buzz-cut head. "Rats!" he said, holding out his clenched fist.

"Ugh!" Betty said, holding out his clenched fist.

"Both ugh and rats," said Charlie, holding out his clenched fist.

Nilly gave the deck of cards a test whack on the edge of the table.

"I'd like to suggest that you guys wear the sleep masks, because this could get really ugly," he said.

"Thanks," Charlie said, and put on one of the British Airways sleep masks.

"Thanks," Betty said, and put on one of the British Airways sleep masks.

"Thanks," Alfie said, and put on one of the British Airways sleep masks.

"Ready?" Nilly asked. "Now I'll just do a little eeny-meeny-miny-moe to myself to see which one of you I'm going to start with, and then we'll get on with it."

The brothers sat speechless, anxiously waiting to find out which of them would be turned into Parmesan cheese first. Charlie was the first one to lose his patience.

"Has he started hitting either of you yet?"

"You fool!" Alfie said. "You would've heard it if he had!"

"How long can it take to do eeny-meeny-miny-moe?" Betty asked.

"A really long time, apparently," Alfie said.

"What are you boys doing?" they heard a deep, familiar voice ask. "And where's the pipsqueak? Did you turn him into Parmesan cheese already?"

They pulled off their sleep masks.

And Mama Crunch was standing in the living-room doorway, holding the grocery bags.

But there was no sign of Nilly. Or his wood-chopping shoe, aiming mitten, or darts.

"He's gone!" Alfie cried.

"He skedaddled!" Betty yelled.

"He vamoosed," Charlie whispered.

This Particular Chapter Has No Title. Hope You Survive.

"YOU CAN LET go now," Nilly said.

He had just stepped into the hotel room and been greeted by a jubilant Doctor Proctor and embraced by a sobbing-with-joy Lisa.

"We were so afraid for you," Lisa sniffled, hugging

her little friend even harder. "We thought you were going to die!"

"I will if you don't let go soon," Nilly said, sounding a little like he was choking.

Lisa sighed and reluctantly let go.

"Tell us what happened!" Doctor Proctor said.

So Nilly did. Of course he might have exaggerated ever so slightly about this or that. But he wouldn't be Nilly if he didn't.

"So you snuck out in the middle of blood knuckles?" Doctor Proctor asked, laughing.

"Yep," Nilly said. "But we have to hurry now, because Rublov is having the gold bars melted down as we speak to turn them into the World Cup trophy!"

"Too late," Lisa said. They looked at her, and she pointed to the TV screen.

And there was Rublov. A tall, blond woman in a short dress was standing behind him. Her hand rested lightly on his shoulder, and there was a diamond the size of your average egg on her ring finger. Ibranaldovez was standing behind her, yawning and looking at the time. A sports reporter was holding a microphone up to Rublov. And behind all that they saw it: the trophy. There was a ribbon around it, and it gleamed solid gold. Lisa turned up the volume.

"How much did you pay for that marvel, Rublov?"

"Her?" Rublov said, gesturing over his shoulder with his thumb. "Or him, farther back there? Mwa-ha-ha! More than I paid for Finland and New Zealand, I'll tell you that."

"Are you planning to score against Rotten Ham on Saturday?" the reporter called to Ibranaldovez.

"Only if he doubles my salary," Ibranaldovez said, pouting and looking at the time again.

"Of course I will, my boy," Rublov said. "Anything else you want?"

"Her," the best soccer player in the world said, pointing to the blonde.

"Fine. As long as *I* get this," Rublov said, patting the big trophy.

The blonde glanced hesitantly from Rublov to Ibranaldovez for a moment before deciding just to smile and go along with it.

Lisa mumbled something and looked offended. Then she turned the volume down again.

"Well," Nilly said. "We can't win every time, but at least we did our best for king and fatherland. When's the next flight back to Oslo?"

"Tomorrow morning at eight thirty," Lisa said. "I guess we might as well start packing."

They started moving slowly toward the bedroom, but stopped when they heard Doctor Proctor clear his throat loudly, "Ahem!" He sat down on the sofa, his face covered in thought wrinkles.

"What is it, Professor?" Lisa asked.

"Oh, I was just thinking."

"We can see that, but *what* are you thinking?" Lisa prodded.

"I was thinking that if I absolutely have to pack, it would be nice to pack the gold we came here to find."

"But the gold is *there*," Lisa said, pointing at the World Cup trophy that the TV happened to be doing a close-up of just then. "And we're *here*."

Nilly lit up. "Does this by any chance call for a robbery?" he asked, cheerfully rubbing his hands together.

"Forget it, Nilly," Lisa said. "That trophy is so heavily guarded that not even your quirky ideas or Doctor Proctor's inventions are enough to get it."

"Lisa's right, as usual," Doctor Proctor said.

"Of course I am," Lisa scoffed. "The only one going home with that gold is the one who wins the stupid World Cup game."

"Exactly," Doctor Proctor said.

Lisa froze and stared uncomprehendingly at Doctor Proctor. He smiled. Then she looked a little less uncomprehending. Then downright scared. "You—don't mean—?"

"I sure do," Doctor Proctor said, beaming.

"Doesn't mean what?" Nilly asked, looking from Lisa to the professor. "Hello? Can somebody please tell me what you guys are talking about?"

"What we're talking about," Lisa said, without taking her eyes off the professor, "is the doctor being a complete, raving lunatic!"

"Yeah, yeah, that's old news," Nilly said. "But in what *way* is he being a lunatic right now?"

"Let me explain it to you," Doctor Proctor said. "Take a seat and pay close attention. . . ."

Doctor Proctor
Goes Crazy
(Or Rather: Even
Crazier Than Usual)

THE SUN HAD just risen over the practice field

Rotten Ham was using. Or Rotten Ham 'n' Potatoes,

which was the team's full official name. Or just "Toes,"

as the team's few local North Central London fans called

them. Or "Stinking Toes," as the team's many foes throughout the rest of London called them. Basically, no one outside London had ever heard of the team, so they didn't call them anything. The reason you either supported Rotten Ham or hated them was that in addition to having the cheapest and therefore worst players in London, they also played the most boring soccer in town. They almost never scored any goals, although on the other hand, they almost never let anyone else score against them either. The reason for this was that they almost always got a toe on the ball before the opposite team could get it into the goal, hence their derogatory nickname, "Stinking Toes."

Today they were practicing scoring goals.

"No, no, no!" Rotten Ham's coach, Eggy Losern, yelled at his players, stomping his rain boots in the grass. "The goal is right there! Do you see it? All righty?"

Eggy Losern came from a long line of tugboat

pilots, but when he had gone to sea, it was as a krill fisherman. While he was on the Antarctic Ocean, he figured out how to lure the krill into the nets using an ingenious zone defense tactic. The goal was to bore them so thoroughly that they ended up falling asleep and swimming right into his seine net like zombies. He was sure this "boring" technique could be used on the soccer field as well, so he resigned his berth on the ship and went ashore. He asked for a chance to coach the worst team in England, Rotten Ham. And since no one else wanted to coach them, he got the job the very same day.

Egg'd been enormously successful. Rotten Ham had gone from being the very worst team in England to being just fourth worst in only two years. And this peculiar krill fisherman, who still dressed like a fisherman in his yellow sou'wester hat and long rubber boots, had gained respect and earned the nickname Krillo. And this year, Krillo and Stinking Toes had stumbled their way all the way to the World Cup finals with a combination of stubbornness, unbelievable luck, and such utterly boring soccer that their opponents had just stood there yawning, and didn't even realize it when Rotten Ham managed to bump the ball into the goal.

But Krillo knew that unfortunately this wouldn't work against the Chelchester City team. Rublov had made that clear. He had seen through Rotten Ham's tactics and was planning to give all his own players two cups of strong coffee before the game started so they would remain wide awake. And besides that, Chelchester City had bought Ibranaldovez, so they would score a goal no matter how zoned Rotten Ham's defense was. Krillo knew that his players were going to have to score more than one goal this time. But how? How?

Krillo lined his players up on the halfway line for the drill and watched them as they each maneuvered a ball to the eighteen-yard box and kicked it. The ball, that is. Or the eighteen-yard box. Not that it mattered what their feet hit, since the balls didn't go into the goal either way.

"You guys, I even took out the goalie!" Krillo grumbled, yanking off his sou'wester. "Look! The goal box is as empty as a lobster pot!"

"It's not *that* easy!" captain Nero Longhands cried, flinging his alarmingly long hands up in the air in despair.

Krillo heard a clear *thunk* behind him. Then a loud whistling sound as some kind of projectile whizzed past him. Then a *whoosh* as the projectile hit the middle of the goal and slid down the net. The projectile bounced a couple of times before coming to rest.

It was a soccer ball.

Krillo slowly turned around.

And saw something very odd.

A tiny little redheaded guy wearing a tweed coat, a

• 256 •

weird, pointy hat made of the same material, and two mismatched shoes, one of them apparently some kind of hand-stitched leather boot. The guy was standing there with his arms at his side and a self-satisfied smile on his lips. Behind him there was a tall, thin, lanky man wearing a penguin suit and what Krillo was willing to bet were swim goggles. The only one of the three who looked more or less normal was standing next to him: a girl with braids, a serious expression, and a soccer ball under her arm.

"Who did that?" Krillo asked.

"Sherl," the man with the swim goggles said, pointing to the little redhead. "Full name Beckadona Hamarooney Sherl, also called 'the Boot of Norway.' And I am his agent, Hamish MacKaroni."

"Get off my practice field!" Krillo ordered, pointing to the exit.

"Ockolmes!" the MacKaroni guy said, and the little girl rolled the ball she was holding to this Beckadona

Hamarooney Sherl, who squinted up one eye, like he was aiming at the goal, and raised the tiny foot wearing the hand-stitched boot as if he were going to shoot. From a hundred feet away without even a running start? Ha! Krillo scoffed and then turned back to his players.

"All righty, now move your balls even closer to the goal, and let's see if—"

Thunk!

Whistle!

Whoosh!

Krillo stared at the ball, which bounced a couple of times inside the goal net, next to the first one. He turned around again.

The redhead was sitting in the grass, blowing on the toe of his hand-stitched boot.

"Well?" MacKaroni said. "Look like a player you could use, eh?"

"How much?" Krillo asked.

"What can you offer?" the player's strange Scottish agent asked.

"Forty-eight pounds and a pair of almost-free cleats."

"As you see, the boy already has his own cleats."

"All righty. Forty-eight pounds plus shoe polish, then."

"You can have them both for that price."

"Both?" Krillo asked, confused.

"Yup." MacKaroni pointed to the girl with the braids. "Sherl and Ockolmes."

"A little girl? Can she play?"

"Not at all," the girl said. "I can't stand the game."

"Shh, Lisa!" the MacKaroni fellow said, and then adjusted his swim goggles. "If I sell Sherl, the girl *has* to be allowed to sit on the reserve bench during the cup finale on Saturday. Sherl gets hot flashes, epilepsy, and bandicoot carbuncles if she and I aren't close by."

"*You're* going to sit on the bench too?"

"Do you have a ball boy?" MacKaroni asked.

"Rotten Ham can't afford things like that," Krillo said with a laugh.

"No problem. I'll be your ball boy," the guy calling himself MacKaroni said, and then pulled a rolled-up sheet of paper out of the inside pocket of his suit jacket. "Here's our contract."

Krillo put on the glasses that were hanging around his neck on a string and read it.

"Well, what do you say?" MacKaroni asked.

"I don't really know . . . ," Krillo said hesitantly.

"What's there to think about?" the little redhead yelled. "Not only do you get three people for the price of one, but also an extra set of tent poles and a bag of charcoal! And that's not all. Since it's such a nice day today, I just decided that I'll throw in a pack—no, not one, *two* packs—of hot chocolate! Now what do you say?"

Krillo stared at the boy. "I say . . . all righty!"

"Yippee!" yelled the normal-looking little girl.

"Yippee!" yelled the abnormal-looking player's agent, Rotten Ham's new ball boy.

"Yippee!" yelled the redheaded Boot of Norway with the baby face.

"No reason to celebrate yet," Krillo said. "Go get your practice gear on, because we're down to the wire now. There's not much time. Saturday is . . . well, now."

The Big Finale

IT WAS A beautiful Saturday in May, and the time was exactly 6:28 in the morning. According to all the approved, government-sanctioned almanacs, that was when the sun was supposed to rise and shine on the Greenwich Observatory and London. But the sun was already a fair ways up into the sky. Because it knew, as all of London's inhabitants did, that today was the day of the final World Cup game, which meant you had to be early to make sure you got a good seat.

So by the time people were pouring into the enormous Wobbley Stadium, the sun had positioned itself so that it could see both goals, and it had no intention of moving until the game was over. Both the long sides and almost both of the short sides were filled with people in blue shirts, blue hats, and blue scarves, and carrying blue banners. They were eating hot dogs and drinking beer and singing songs about how good Chelchester City was. The only place that wasn't completely blue was the very bottom of the stands, behind the one goal. There was a small group wearing white there. Those were the people singing about how Rotten Ham wasn't actually so bad. At least not on a good day. A guy named Tony was leading their singing. He was not wearing a shirt. He was the local tattoo artist on Rotten Ham Road and had the team's club logo—a piece of rotten ham—tattooed across his whole chest, along with the team's name: ROTTEN HAM FOREVER. Unfortunately, the letters were left-right reversed, since Tony had tattooed them on himself using a mirror.

Tony and the others sang:

"Toes, my Toes, you're not exactly England's rose
But the game hasn't started yet, and who knows
We may not lose this time, let's see how it goes
So don't give up, cheer up, my mighty Toes!"

Krillo was sitting in front of his players in the locker room under the stands, listening to the song. They could hear all the blue-clad fans laughing themselves silly at the fairly uninspired lyrics. The Rotten Ham players were sitting with their heads in their hands, staring at the floor. Some of them were quaking like aspen leaves, because they'd never played in front of such a large audience before. And the game was going to be broadcast live on TV around the world! Yikes!

"All righty," Krillo said, adjusting his sou'wester and rubbing his hands together. "It's almost time for the kickoff. Are we ready, Toes?"

No response.

"Are we ready, Toes?" Krillo repeated. "Nero? Answer me!"

"Uh . . . ," Nero began, pushing up his captain's armband, which had slid down his long, skinny arm yet again. "Very ready. I think."

"That's how it should be!" Krillo yelled. "That's the attitude I want to see! Any of you not looking forward to this, anyone scared to go out onto that crummy little field?"

All the players—except the tiny redheaded one—nodded.

"I think you guys misunderstood my question," Krillo said. "Let me put it more clearly. Do any of you wish we hadn't made it this far, to the finals?"

"Yes," all the players responded, apart from . . . well, you know which one.

"Really?" Krillo said, irritated. "You'd rather we just went home and forgot the whole thing instead of going out there and taking a pounding from the best team in all of England and the most expensive player in the world?"

"Yes!" all the players cried in unison, even the tiny redhead, although just because he'd gotten carried away by their conviction.

Krillo's head sank into his hands in despair. "Fools!" he yelled, outraged. "The correct answer is 'no!' That's three out of three you got wrong! All righty, let's give it one more try. . . ."

"No!" all the players yelled.

Krillo rolled his eyes. "I haven't even asked the question yet! All righty, let's forget the questions. Here comes your pep talk now, so pay close attention and imagine inspirational music, rising to a crescendo like in a Hollywood movie, all righty?"

Krillo stood up, cleared his throat, and closed his eyes in concentration. "Let's see. Yes, here's how it goes: We shall fight on the seas and oceans, we shall fight in the air, we shall fight on the beaches, we shall—"

"Excuse me?" Nero Longhands asked.

"Yes?" Krillo said.

"In the schedule it says our game is at Wobbley. What's all this about oceans and beaches? Are we in the wrong stadium?"

"Fool!" Krillo said, stomping to express his anger, although his rubber fisherman's boot didn't make much noise.

The door opened, and there stood a middle-aged man with thinning hair, wearing shorts that flapped loosely around a pair of unbelievably skinny thighs.

"Get out!" Krillo growled. "I'm giving my players a pep talk here!"

"And I'm here to tell you that if you're not out on the field in ten seconds, the match is going to start without you," the man said.

Krillo glared at him and said, "You're what?"

"Everyone's waiting for you guys," the man with the thinning hair and thin thighs said.

"I think that's the referee," the girl with the braids said.

Krillo glanced suspiciously at his watch. Tapped it. Put it up to his ear. "Hmm, looks like my watch stopped. All righty, I'll have to give you your pep talk after the game, boys. And . . . uh, girl. Let's start trouncing them, Toes!"

And with that all the players ran out the door, through the players' tunnel, and out into the tremendous noise in Wobbley Stadium.

Doctor Proctor (aka Hamish MacKaroni) and Lisa (aka Ockolmes) sat down next to Krillo on the bench by the sideline.

"Where are the other substitutes?" Doctor Proctor asked.

"What substitutes?" Krillo asked. "You don't think we can afford to pay people who don't play, do you?"

"What if someone gets . . . uh, injured?" Lisa asked.

"They're not allowed to get hurt," Krillo said. "Could you quit bugging me now so I can concentrate?"

Ibranaldovez was standing in the middle of the field, ready for the kickoff, but looking down at Nilly.

"Seriously?" he sneered. "You're going to *play*? I thought you were the mascot. I'm going to have to pick you out of my cleats after the game."

And then, at exactly forty-three seconds after four o'clock, forty-three seconds later than planned, a whistle blow started the big World Cup finale.

THE GAME CLOCK had just passed forty-three minutes when Krillo moaned in despair, because this couldn't be happening. Chelchester City had had the ball the whole time and they had made two offside goals, three goalpost shots, eighteen corner kicks, and the bookmakers were giving them five-hundred-to-one odds of winning. In other words, it was a miracle that the score was still 0–0. Ibranaldovez shot, and Krillo leaped into the air with excitement on the sideline as the ball bounced off the crossbar. Krillo came back down again on the very end of the bench, flipping it up and launching Lisa into the air so that she landed again with a little "Hiccup!"

"Two minutes until halftime," Krillo said, mostly to himself. "If we can just keep it 0–0 until then! Please, oh, please!"

The Rotten Ham 'n' Potatoes goalkeeper passed the ball to Nero Longhands.

"Get the ball out to that little redheaded guy!" Krillo yelled.

"Beckadona Hamarooney Sherl," Doctor Proctor said.

"Whatever. Just get him the ball!"

Nero tried, but it wasn't so easily accomplished, this feat. First he had to gain control of the ball and then send it where he wanted it. Not to mention all these guys dressed in blue all over him all the time. They were really pushy! But now he saw the little redheaded boy who'd been standing in the center circle for the whole game, waiting for the ball. Yes, that little Beckumoonie Shirley or whatever his name was had even lain down in the grass for a while when Chelchester City was giving them their worst. The little guy had plucked a blade of grass, stuck it between his teeth, and lain down with his hands clasped behind his head, staring up at the blue sky.

Nero aimed for the little boy and kicked at the ball, but ended up kicking the turf just behind it instead. And suddenly his leg was in Ibranaldovez's legs.

"Tackle!" Krillo yelled.

And Nero lunged forward, shut his eyes, and tackled Ibranaldovez.

Which is to say: He wasn't entirely sure if he'd tackled Ibranaldovez.

Apparently he'd tackled the air where Ibranaldovez had just been standing a second before, because when he opened his eyes again, he heard a roar of cheering from the stands and saw Ibranaldovez on his way back with his hands up in victory. It might have just been an accident that Ibranaldovez happened to step on Nero's hand as he went by.

"No!" Krillo screamed. "No! No!"

"Well, well," Doctor Proctor said.

The teams each moved back to their sides of the field again. Rotten Ham put the ball on the midline and waited for the referee to blow his whistle and start play again. Nilly yawned, spit his blade of grass out, and walked over to the ball along with his teammates.

"Watch this," Doctor Proctor told Krillo, who'd pulled his sou'wester down over his face.

But Krillo wasn't watching. Instead he was staring at the inside of his sou'wester, dreaming that he was back on his krill-fishing boat in the Antarctic Ocean, teeth chattering as they hauled in the net, pulling yet another big catch onboard. He should have stuck with that! Not come to this gloomy country where everything was sorrow and . . .

Thunk!

. . . miserable . . .

Whistle!

. . . wretchedness?

Judging from what Krillo could *hear* as he stared at the inside of his sou'wester, there was cheering. Not as loud as before, but if he wasn't mistaken, he thought he heard a guy named Tony singing something like, "Toes, my Toes, you're not exactly England's rose . . ."

He opened his eyes and saw a pile of players wearing white. Eventually a little redheaded guy crawled out of the pile and ran over to the stands, blowing kisses to the crowd, both the ones wearing blue and the ones in white. And Krillo also saw the world's best soccer player's eyes about to pop out of his head.

"From midfield!" MacKaroni, the new ball boy, cried excitedly. "Did you *see* that?"

And then, with a score of 1–1, the referee blew his whistle and it was halftime.

A Short Interlude

"YOU JUST HAVE to do that one more time," Doctor Proctor whispered to Nilly as Krillo spoke, diagrammed, and pointed to the whiteboard in the locker room.

"I know, but I'll never get the ball," Nilly said. "The only time would be at the kickoff after *they've* scored!"

"Be patient," Lisa whispered. "We have to win! We're heading straight to the airport with the trophy from here!"

"Yeah, about that," Nilly said. "Did you guys get the fake trophy from Madame Tourette's Wax Museum?"

"Yeah, of course," Lisa said. "I'm going to have it in my suitcase, and I'll be waiting in the players' tunnel right after the game. And you remember what you have to do?"

"Yep," Nilly said. "After I accept the adulations of the crowd for having more or less single-handedly determined the outcome of the World Cup final with my fantastic shot and the ladies are begging me for kisses and——"

"Get to the point!" Lisa said.

"Yeah, sure. Holding the trophy, I will be carried to the locker room on the shoulders of my teammates, and as we enter the players' tunnel——"

"I'll turn off the lights," Doctor Proctor said.

"And in the darkness, Nilly will toss the trophy down to me," Lisa said. "And I'll swap it out, toss the fake trophy back up to you, and put the real one, which is made of the Bank of Norway's gold, into the suitcase."

"Then we catch the first flight home to Oslo," Doctor Proctor said. "And get home just in time so that the trophy can be melted back down again into a gold bar, put back into the vault, and the inspection will go off without a hitch."

"And I will be carried through the streets of Oslo on people's shoulders as girls throw red roses at me and burst into tears when they realize that I can't marry them all unless the king passes a new law that says that I, Nilly, am actually allowed to marry——"

"LET'S GET ON WITH IT, THEN!" Krillo yelled. "And don't wait too long to start trouncing them, please!"

Nilly certainly had no intention of doing that.

Back at the
Final World Cup Game

NO, NILLY HAD no intention of waiting at all.

Because Rotten Ham had the kickoff in the second half.

Nero Longhands nudged the ball to Nilly, who stood ready, his foot raised.

Thunk!

"I made a little adjustment last night, you know,"

Doctor Proctor (aka MacKaroni) told Krillo.

Whistle!

"I moved the heel, which is actually designed for chopping wood, up to the toe of the shoe."

Whoosh!

"Really smart, huh?" Doctor Proctor said.

It was 2–1 Rotten Ham! Cheers erupted in the tiny Rotten Ham fan section and the players once again buried Nilly under a pile of sweaty bodies.

Nilly emerged from the pile and once again ran toward the stands, blowing kisses left and right. He thought he even noticed some of the blue-clad female spectators looking like they really wanted to blow kisses back to him, but of course they didn't dare for fear of how the other blue whiners would penalize such disloyal behavior.

Nero patted Nilly on the head. "I'm sure I'll be able to get you the ball a few times," he said. "We're going to win this!"

"Definitely," Nilly said, concentrating on pulling off a rather decent moonwalk over the grass, which is no small feat when you're wearing one hand-stitched boot and one soccer cleat. When the cheers subsided and they were ready to let Chelchester City kick off, Nilly heard a voice right by his ear:

"Is that your sister, that ugly girl on the bench over there?"

"Hey, no one calls Lisa ugly!" Nilly said, turning around.

It was Ibranaldovez. He was sneering down at Nilly. "Your sister is the ugliest girl I've ever seen, and I've seen a lot of girls. She's uglier than the village I come from at low tide, and that's ugly! And dumb! She's dumber than one of those trees you put in your living room around Christmastime, what are they called again? Whatever. Those trees are really, really dumb, and that's how dumb she is. At least. No, actually, she's even dumber. Ha-ha! Did you hear that? She's dumber than one of those

tree-thingies! And ugly! Did I mention the part about low tide back home? Why's your face so red, huh?"

Nilly felt his head boiling. No one—*no one!*—was allowed to talk about Lisa that way! Or any of his other friends! Not even Eva, who actually *was* his sister! Nilly's first thought was that he should ram Ibranaldovez in the chest, but the problem was that he only came up to the man's knees.

So he kicked Ibranaldovez instead. On the butt. It just sort of happened.

Thunk!

A whistling noise ran through the crowd as they watched the best soccer player in the world soaring through the air, flying over the field and up into the stands. And a groan as he landed in the VIP section.

"Ibranaldovez just landed right in Maximus Rublov's lap!" a radio reporter screamed into his microphone.

"The ref is giving the double-scoring Beckadona Hamarooney Sherl a red card!" a TV reporter howled.

"I'm sorry," Nilly said, flopping down onto the bench next to Krillo, Doctor Proctor, and Lisa. For once he looked truly crushed.

"It might not make that much difference," Krillo said. "We're ahead 2–1, and we're usually good at defense. This might work!"

"I mean," Nilly said, "I'm sorry I kicked that idiot. I could have hurt him."

"I hope you really did!" Krillo said. "Would you tickle the devil! I can see him moving around up there!"

And sure enough, Ibranaldovez was back on the field ten minutes later. He was rubbing one butt cheek a little, but seemed more excited than ever to score a goal.

Two shots that hit the goalposts and three saves in a row later, Krillo looked at the clock and determined there was only one minute left. The Chelchester fans were moaning in despair, pulling out clumps of hair, and biting their fingernails almost all the way to the second knuckle.

"If we can ward off this corner shot, we win!" Krillo whispered.

The corner shot came in high, in front of the goal. Two players leaped into the air: Rotten Ham's goalie and Ibranaldovez.

"This is great!" Krillo whispered. "He won't be able to head the ball higher than our goalie can reach!"

Then, as if he'd been kneed in the stomach, the Rotten Ham goalie grabbed his stomach and doubled over. And another hand rose up over the goalie's head. A very particular hand. Ibranaldovez's hand. And it *hit* the ball.

Whoosh!

"Goal!" the Chelchester fans screamed.

"Handball!" the Rotten Ham fans screamed.

"A particular hand!" Maximus Rublov screamed.

"Volleyball!" Krillo screamed.

"Goal," the referee said, and pointed to the middle line.

Ibranaldovez ran victoriously toward the stands, stopping in front of the Rotten Ham bench to lean over to Nilly and whisper triumphantly, "That didn't hurt at all, so there!"

Our friends and Krillo sat staring straight ahead, stunned, as the referee let Rotten Ham take the kickoff before blowing his whistle to end the game.

2–2.

"What now?" Lisa asked.

"Extra time," Krillo said. "And you need to go warm up."

"Me?" Lisa asked.

"You're our only substitute," Krillo said, nodding toward the goal where their goalie was lying on the ground, clutching his stomach as he was helped onto a stretcher.

Lisa gulped. She was about to get exactly what she'd asked for: to have the whole world watching her.

Extra Time
(Tell Me, Will It
Never End?)

"I DON'T WANT to go out there and—and—make
a fool of myself in front of the whole world!" Lisa said.
She kicked at the grass in irritation and looked up at
the sold-out stands and all the TV cameras. "If my feet
were small enough to fit into that boot, maybe then
there would be some point to my playing."

"I know," Doctor Proctor said, watching the referee walk toward the center circle to start the extra time. "But we have to try whatever we can to win this game! If there's no winner, there'll be a rematch next Saturday, and that'll be too late."

"Please, Lisa!" Nilly said. "At least you don't have to stand in the goal." He pointed to the goal, where Nero Longhands was standing, wearing gloves and the goalie's jersey.

Nero had never been goalie before, but since no one else on the Rotten Ham team had either, Krillo had done a quick eeny-meeny-miny-moe-holy-moley-pick-a-goalie. And Nero had lost.

The referee started the game again by blowing his whistle. Lisa was playing left back. Krillo had said she should try to get in the way of the guys in the blue as much as she could and that they didn't really expect anything else from her.

But every once in a while it's funny how fate can

step in and put a person in just the right place in this world, a place no one had the slightest idea they truly belonged. And I'm not talking about Lisa now. The few times Lisa got anywhere near the ball, she was pretty much running the wrong way, looking the wrong way, or not really understanding how a ball rolls, bounces, and sort of generally behaves.

I'm talking about Nero Longhands.

"Did you see that save?!" the radio reporter screamed to the sideline commentator after Ibranaldovez headed the ball right toward the very bottom corner of the goal. But in one tiger leap, Nero was there, stretching out one of those unbelievably long arms of his to put his hand between the ball and the ground and then hammering it *over* the crossbar. "Gordon, I haven't seen anything like this since—since—"

"Get Longhands on the national team NOW!" the TV reporter howled as Nero saved a super-hard shot with ease. And the Chelchester fans kept groaning, pulling out their hair, and chomping on their finger-nails as Nero caught, saved, and wiped his hands. And even here, before you know the outcome of this match, I will give you the good news. Because the good news is that Nero Longhands had a long and prestigious career as the national team's goalkeeper. The not-quite-so-good news, well, the downright bad news, was that this game was almost over and there was *no* sign that Rotten Ham was going to cross the midline and approach Chelchester's goal.

"We have to do something!" Doctor Proctor cried in desperation. "There's only a minute and a half left in the game!"

"I hate clocks," Nilly mumbled.

Just then the ball rolled toward Lisa, who was standing way over by the sideline in front of the bench. It stopped right in front of her feet, and she stared down at it.

"Come on, Lisa!" Nilly yelled from the bench. "Get

going! Do a Cruyff Turn, a camel feint, a nutmeg, then a bicycle kick! It's not *that* hard!"

"It's not?" Lisa said, cautiously raising her foot. She didn't get any farther than that, because Ibranaldovez came flying through the air, cleats first, right then. His cleats hit both Lisa and the ball, causing them both to fly off the field and hit the ads with a sickening crash.

"Red card!" Krillo screamed angrily, leaping up off the bench. "Life-long imprisonment! Electric chair!"

But the referee just gave them a free kick.

Lisa opened her eyes and looked up to see three Nillys and three Doctor Proctors all looking down at her, seeming very concerned.

"Does it hurt anywhere?" Nilly asked.

"Only all over," Lisa said. "And could you please stop being in triplicate?"

"You just hit your head a little," Doctor Proctor said. "Lie still, Lisa, I'll go get—"

"Lie still?" Lisa said, irritatedly kicking away the

advertising banner, which was half covering her, and getting up. "We have a game to win!" Then she passed out and fell right back down on her butt again.

"Lie still, you have a concussion, and it's too late to do anything about the game anyway. Here, drink a little water," Doctor Proctor said.

But instead of taking the bottle, Lisa furrowed her brow in concentration.

"We have to take that trophy home with us *today*," she said.

"She didn't just hit her head a *little* bit," Nilly muttered.

"That free kick, it's ours, right?" Lisa asked.

"Yes, but my dear Lisa, even if I had a wood-chopping shoe that fit you, it's quite a ways down *our* half of the field."

Lisa got up. "Do you remember what you packed as we were leaving home?"

"Uh, yeah?"

"Give me the bag of the stuff that I foolishly didn't want you to bring."

"You mean . . . ," Doctor Proctor began.

"She means . . . ," Nilly said.

"Hurry!" Lisa moaned.

Doctor Proctor ran back to the bench, opened the suitcase, found the bag, and brought it to Lisa, who resolutely opened it and poured the contents into her mouth. Nilly licked the bag to make sure all the powder was gone. Then Lisa marched over to Krillo.

"I want to take that free kick," she said.

Krillo sighed and shrugged. "All righty. It'll be the last kick anyway. The referee is just blowing his whistle now."

"HELLO!" THE RADIO reporter said. "It looks like Rotten Ham is planning to let that little girl take the last kick in what has been a dramatic final game.

She's taking position. With her back to the ball, actually. Is she planning on wrapping this up with a heel kick? Well, why not?"

LISA LOOKED UP at the stands. Saw all those faces staring at her. She wasn't the least bit nervous anymore. Her only thought was that she didn't care if it seemed impossible, because she *could* do this! Because she was Lisa, the one and only Lisa. She felt a bubbling in her stomach. She knew it would come soon, and she started counting down: six, five, four . . .

She saw the referee raise the whistle to his lips, and she bent over all the way so her butt was pointing right at the ball. She remembered what Nilly had explained, that if her butt was pointing down toward the ground too much, she would launch herself into the air, like a fartonaut.

Two, one . . .

Then it came. The explosion. The one that comes after you swallow a whole bag of Doctor Proctor's fartonaut powder.

The radio reporter screamed, "It almost looked like her heel didn't make contact with the ball at all, and yet the ball is flying off like a projectile!"

"But it's heading straight for Chelchester's goal, so the goalie is bound to catch it," his co-commentator said. "There, he caught it."

"But look, Gordon! There was so much force to the kick that the ball's taking the goalie with it. . . . Wow! All the way *into* the goal and . . . the whole net is ripping!"

"That's the worst I've seen!"

"That's the best I've seen, Gordon!"

"But that's a goal! 3–2 Rotten Ham!"

"And there! The referee blew his whistle. The game is over!"

"Rotten Ham 'n' Potatoes has won it, Gordon!"

"Lisa!" Nilly howled, leaping up and down.

"Best in the world! Lisa!" Doctor Proctor cheered.

"Ockolmes!" Krillo roared, running out onto the field just as fast as his fisherman's boots could carry him.

"Toes, my Toes!" sang Tony and the other fans dressed in white over in the corner.

And then for a while they all ran around hugging and telling each other that it was really true: They'd won the World Cup at Wobbley Stadium!

And after Nero Longhands and the other players on the team had gone up to the queen and picked up their awards, they carried Lisa around the stadium on their shoulders while she held up the big trophy.

"Carry me to the locker room," she commanded, clutching the trophy.

And when they were in the middle of the players' tunnel, right as they passed the spot where Nilly was standing with an innocent smile and an open suitcase,

someone—probably a guy in swim goggles—turned off the lights so it went dark.

There was screaming and yowling and tumult, but when the lights came on again a moment later, Lisa was still sitting up on her teammates' shoulders. And the trophy she was holding was so identical to the one she'd been holding a few seconds earlier that it didn't occur to anyone that it might be a different trophy.

And while the players were drinking champagne and celebrating in the locker room, a black London cab was flooring it to the airport. And the cab contained a driver, three happy people we're very familiar with, and a suitcase containing a gleaming World Cup trophy with a ribbon around it.

Jell-O. What Else?

IT WAS MONDAY. Oslo was bathed in May sunshine. The bell had just rung after their last class, and Lisa and Nilly were walking home together.

"What was it like to come home and not have your own room anymore?" Lisa asked.

"That's what was so weird," Nilly said. "Eva had moved all her stuff back out, and she said I could have my room back."

"Oh?"

"Yeah. She even gave me a hug. And said she'd missed me a tiny bit. I'm afraid she might even hug me again sometime," Nilly said with a shudder.

"Well, but isn't that good?" Lisa asked. "I've heard that a hug from your sister is one of the nicest things in the world."

"Being hugged up against such large red zits?" Nilly said. "Good thing I bought that zit cream for her at the airport in London, huh?"

"Is that why you had to borrow money from Doctor Proctor?"

"Yeah, I couldn't come home without even so much as an English tea bag, could I? I'll save up the money and pay Doctor Proctor back."

"Hmm," Lisa said.

"What do you mean, 'hmm'?" Nilly asked, since he knew Lisa well enough to be able to hear that this wasn't just a *hmm* hmm.

"You guys argue all the time," Lisa said. "But you know what? I think deep down inside you love each other some after all."

"Me? Love? That witch, *Eva*?" Nilly scoffed, rolling his eyes. But Lisa just smiled wisely, as if to say he wasn't fooling her with that act.

They turned onto Cannon Avenue, and as they did so a large black limousine pulled up next to them and stopped, and the back door opened.

"Lisa and Nilly! Hop in!"

A man they'd met before was sitting in the backseat.

"We're on our way to see Doctor Proctor," the king of Norway said. "Congratulations on a mission well done. The inspection was this morning, and the World Bank was happy with everything."

"Well, we didn't have time to melt it down, so they did think it was a little odd that Norway's national gold reserve was shaped like a big trophy," the driver said, smiling into the rearview mirror.

"Hi, Helge," Lisa said.

"One of the inspectors picked it up and thought it felt surprisingly light for solid gold," the man in the front passenger seat said. "But we explained that the trophy always feels light after a victory."

"Hi, Hallgeir," Nilly said.

"And we just received a phone call from London from our colleagues in Her Royal Highness's Even More Secret Service. They still don't have any proof that Rublov and the Crunch Brothers stole the gold, but they arrested Rublov anyway."

"Why?" Nilly asked.

Helge and Hallgeir both chuckled a little before they responded, "A bank employee told the police that Rublov threatened her with a gun when he forcibly deposited Monopoly money into her bank. And that the bank has surveillance video to prove it."

"Plus, there were witnesses who saw Rublov rob an old lady and her baby in Hyde Park."

"Plus, he apparently hung on to the back of a sightseeing bus, stealing a ride without paying his fare."

"He's going to be in jail for a good while."

They pulled over in front of Doctor Proctor's overgrown yard, and when they pushed open the crooked gate, they saw a big banner draped between the pear trees.

JELL-O FESTIVAL.

And there they all were, under the banner. Doctor Proctor and Juliette Margarine, Eva and Nilly's mom, Lisa's commandant father and her mother, Mrs. Strobe from school, and Gregory Galvanius.

And on the picnic table behind them was the biggest Jell-O mold any of them had ever seen.

Juliette was carrying a tray of champagne and pear soda around, and once they'd all helped themselves, the king chimed his spoon on the side of his glass and turned to them.

"My dear subjects . . ."

Mrs. Strobe cleared her throat, raising an eyebrow and giving the king a stern look over the top of her glasses.

"Uh, I mean my dear fellow citizens," the king hurriedly corrected himself. "And dear friends. Yes, most especially friends . . ."

Mrs. Strobe nodded approvingly, and the king continued:

"I have a joyous announcement to make. It comes from my third cousin, or perhaps she's my second cousin . . . a few even claim she's my first cousin. Unfortunately, a few things happened that make it slightly unclear. . . ."

Mrs. Strobe cleared her throat again.

"Anyhow, to the point!" the king hurriedly said. "The queen of England has decided to name Lisa the Jack of Spades of New South Wales for her extraordinary performance during the finale at Wobbley. And Doctor Proctor will be dubbed a knight of the third-rate order for restoring the Empire to greatness with his invention. England is planning to launch its first fartonaut into space next month!"

Everyone present clapped and cried "hurra," which is Norwegian for hooray. After that everyone turned and looked at Nilly.

"Sorry, Nilly," the king said. "The queen didn't really think it was appropriate to honor someone who's famous for having kicked the world's best soccer player into the stands."

Everyone laughed.

"Yeah, yeah," Nilly said, laughing with them. "At least I got a little notoriety."

"Exactly," the king said with a knowing wink.

Everyone waited anxiously to hear what would come next. But the king took his time, sniffling, adjusting his shirt collar a little, taking a sip from his glass. Until Mrs. Strobe cleared her throat in warning.

"Right," the king said. "It turns out that after they were done making the new wax figures for Madame Tourette's Wax Museum this year, they had a little bit of wax left over. Not much. Not enough for your average prime minister, for example. But enough for a little guy who already has his own fan clubs over in England, someone everyone is curious about, wondering *whatever happened to him*? But all they know about him is that he called himself Beckadona Hamarooney Sherl."

"They're going to make a wax figure of me!" Nilly squealed. "I'm famous!"

"In a way," the king said. "But since you were at

Wobbley on an assignment of a rather secret nature, unfortunately, you can never tell *anyone* that you are Sherl."

"Rats!" Nilly said.

"And so I suggest a secret toast to Sherl!" the king proposed.

Everyone laughed and raised their glasses to Nilly, who bowed low before draining the pear soda from his glass in one long gulp. Followed by a not insignificant burp.

Then they sat down at the table.

And while they slowly consumed yard after yard of the best Jell-O any of them had ever eaten, Lisa whispered to Nilly, asking him if he was sure he had managed to swap out the trophy in the players' tunnel. And Nilly responded that it was true, that type of on-the-fly, pitch-dark trophy exchange was not for amateurs, but he wasn't Nilly for nothing. Was he?

Lisa studied her friend thoughtfully as he arrogantly

stuffed another foot or so of Jell-O into his mouth.

"But you're *totally* sure that—" she began.

She didn't get any response, because just then they heard a voice yelling and the distant hum of an engine. Everyone looked around, unable to place where the sounds were coming from. Until someone happened to look up. And there, high above the top of the pear tree, they saw a triangular shape approaching.

"Look at me! I'm Petter! I'm the one and only Petter, and a heck of a Petter I am!"

"Petter!" Lisa called up to him. "Who's that with you?"

"Huh?"

"The girl next to you?" Lisa clarified.

"Oh, right. This is Petronella. She's the one and only Petronella! A heck of a Petronella! She's the one who added the engine to the hang glider. A real Hillman engine! We flew straight into the headwind! Is there any Jell-O left, Doctor?"

And there was.

And as our friends ate, laughed, and told their unbelievable stories, and Nilly tried to teach everyone the Toes song, the spring sun sank behind the crooked blue house at the very end of Cannon Avenue.

And with that, we call the game over for now.

THE END

OR . . .

MEANWHILE, ACROSS THE North Sea, three brothers were playing poker in the city called London. And their mother covered her ears as they yelled things to one another like:

"It is too true! You got a flush. That means you have to flush it down the toilet, so I win! International rules!"

"But then I jack your ace, so now it's my ace!"

"Stick out your knuckles!"

"You boys are driving me crazy," their mother muttered, escaping to the kitchen to make more Birmingham pudding.

IN A SMALL shack of a clubhouse, Krillo yelled for Nero to come help him lift the trophy into the trophy case, which had been empty ever since Rotten Ham had been founded a hundred years earlier.

"It's almost weird," Krillo groaned as they lifted. "That a trophy should be so heavy!"

AND LONG AFTER the sun had set in Norway and England, the party was over, and you and I had gone to bed, a guy by the name of Nilsen woke up when the phone next to his bed rang.

"Yes?" he said with a yawn.

"Is this the host of Norway's Biggest Liar?"

"Yes," Nilsen said, wondering where he'd heard the caller's voice before.

"I have an anonymous tip for you. Do you remember that guy named Nilly, who you had on your show?"

"The one who said he was Napoléon and saved the world from moon monsters?" Nilsen said, chuckling. "He's not easily forgotten."

"I know," the voice said. "But I just want to give you this supersecret tip that he's Beckadona Hamarooney Sherl."

"The player who scored the goal against Chelchester in the World Cup finals and just disappeared?"

"Yes. Unfortunately, he had more important things to do than hang out in England and revel in the glory, becoming rich and famous and running away from English girls who wanted to kiss him. But you might find it interesting to know that Nilly,

aka Sherl, is going to be on display as a wax figure in Madame Tourette's Wax Museum."

"This is totally unbelievable!" Nilsen said, thinking that there was something very familiar about that voice.

"You could mention this on your stupid show, that that Nilly had the goods after all. Good night."

"I see. This wouldn't happen to be Nilly I'm talking to, would it?"

But the caller had already hung up.